AT GREAT PRICE

PRICE

The Story of Tamsen Donner

By Mabel Chapman

Published by:
Mabel Chapman
16631 Dearborn St.
North Hills, CA 91343

Cover design by Joanne Ronce

©Mabel Chapman 1992

ISBN 0-9634580-0-0

Forward

At Great Price is an historical novel. It is the true story of the last year in the life of Tamsen Donner (1802-1847); writer, educator, feminist, wife and mother. It is the story of her experiences on a cut-off trail to California and while snowbound on the eastern slopes of the Sierra Nevadas. She was one of a group of emigrants heading west from St. Louis and elsewhere to seek a new life in California. It is also the story of courageous personal choices made, for better or worse, out of a sense of commitment to another human being.

The fate of this splinter group of pioneers, popularly known as the "Donner Party" has been called "California's Greatest Tragedy" and is well known particularly among California school children studying the state's history. The story was well known to Northern Californians shortly after its occurrence. However, only two years later, in 1849, gold was discovered at Sutter's Mill and the frenzy of the Gold Rush overshadowed the tale of the Donner Party.

Contrary to common perception, the party was not lead by Tamsen's husband George Donner, a popular well-to-do farmer and businessman retiring to California to spend his leisure under the grape arbors of the golden state. It should be called "Hastings' Deserted Emigrant Party" because they chose to part company from a larger group heading to Oregon after reading of an alternate route promoted by Lansford Hastings. Hastings urged his short cut by a book, lectures and posters along the trail in which he offered to lead emigrants to California if they would leave the Oregon Trail and meet him at Fort Bridger, saving one hundred miles of travel.

Tamsen was forty-five at the time of this episode in her life. She had lost her family and then had made a suitable middle aged marriage to George, also widowed. At the time of her marriage to him her expectations about love and devotion were naturally not great. Her dream was to start a finishing school for girls when she reached California. She was an educated woman, generous with her knowledge and interested in continual learning. There was much she would learn on this journey to California.

Based in fact and painstakingly accurate in terms of historical figures and events, the detailed conversations among the people in this story are nonetheless fictionalized. How do I know these things? The author, Mabel Chapman, is my grandmother.

Leslie Chapman Young

AT GREAT PRICE

Chapter 1

A shout of "Donner it is. Donner it is," arose among the group of men in a circle of covered wagons which were camped by Little Creek on the Oregon-California trail.

Tamsen Donner was gloomy and depressed that morning of July 20, 1846. She had taken her basket and gone a little distance from the camp, picking lupin for her botany collection. With her were her three daughters, Frances, Georgia, and Eliza.

"I wonder what's up," she said to her daughters. "What has your father or Jake done?"

Then she heard James Reed's voice. "Come over to the wagon. We have to drink to that."

James Reed stood at the side entrance of his elaborately built covered wagon, christened the Pioneer Palace Car by his stepdaughter, Virginia. He brought bottles of wine and brandy from the storage level of the wagon.

Again there was shouting. "To Donner. To Donner. To George Donner, our leader."

Tamsen was disturbed. It looked as if the die was cast in favor of the emigrants leaving the party led by ex-governor Boggs along the Oregon trail and taking the cutoff by Fort Bridger and Salt Lake. That cutoff trail had been recommended by Lansford Hastings in his book *The Emigrant's Guide to Oregon and California*.

Elizabeth Donner, Jacob's wife and sister-in-law of Tamsen, came hurrying to meet her.

"Did you hear?" asked Elizabeth, "They are making

George the leader."

Tamsen nodded solemnly. "I suppose that means that they have made up their minds."

"It's a wonder they didn't make Mr. Reed the leader," said Elizabeth.

Tamsen winced. She knew it was true that James Reed was a very dynamic and forceful man. Her sense of loyalty was to her husband, a man with a gentle and charitable spirit, a man who had been Uncle George to neighbors back in Illinois.

"But see," said Elizabeth eagerly, "Now that George is leader, what he says goes. Talk to him and try to persuade him to go with Governor Boggs. Look," she waved toward the northwest, "all morning they have been going in that direction. There must be hundreds of wagons following Governor Boggs."

"They are not all going to California. Many are going to Oregon."

"Yes I know," said Elizabeth. "But lots of our friends are going that way. I don't know many of these people waiting around here."

"Neither do I. Of course, I know the Reeds and the Eddys. I just met Mrs. Breen."

"The Breens have as big an outfit as each of us, three wagons and a good number of cattle and horses. Oh, like me, Mrs. Breen has one girl and six boys."

"Well, I'll go and try again to talk George out of going by the shortcut," said Tamsen.

With her basket on her arm she went back to her family wagon. George, with a wide smile on his face, joined her.

He said, "Well it's all settled. We are going by the Salt Lake cutoff."

"Jim Clyman says it's dangerous," said Tamsen.

George grinned and said teasingly, "You womenfolk all want to believe Clyman. He's handsome and dashing on horseback. What's that poem? I've heard you recite it when the neighborhood book club met at our house. I remember when my older girls were on school programs they used to recite it, too, something about Lochinvar came a dashing out of the west."

At the time George met Tamsen he was a widower with grown children and grandchildren. In the seven years of his marriage to Tamsen he liked to tease her, to refer to himself as an old man. He had been fifty-six at the time of their marriage. He liked to refer to her as a little young thing. Little she was, scarcely a hundred pounds, but she had not been young. She had been thirty-eight at the time of their marriage. For years she had been a teacher in a young ladies' finishing school. George had another theme for teasing: her education and her success in writing. Even on this trip she was writing and sketching for a book about the flowers of the west, and as this morning, she was gathering botany specimens.

George said, "You had better get ready to leave. Jake's wagons are ready and Reed will be ready in an hour. It's getting late. Governor Boggs pulled out early this morning. We should have left earlier, too. We can't expect that Lansford Hastings will wait forever for us at Fort Bridger."

George joined the men's group. In answer to Elizabeth's questioning, Tamsen shook her head.

She said, "Well, we better round up our little ones. Look, they are over by that creek, throwing rocks to see the water splash." Raising her voice she called to her stepdaughters, Eliza and Leanna, who were returning from gathering flowers. "Girls, your father says we are about to leave. You better get your horses tethered to the wagon."

Tamsen and Elizabeth were joined by Eleanor Eddy and Mrs. Breen as they went to their shouting and laughing children.

After Eleanor captured her three-year-old Jimmie she asked, "Mrs. Donner, are we really going by the cutoff? My husband says we are going whichever way Mr. Donner and Mr. Reed go. Why is the cutoff shorter?"

Tamsen picked up a stick and scratched a triangle in the dirt with the wide angle at the top. "Here we are at Little Sandy," she said, pointing the stick at the lower corner. She trailed the stick along the line going northwest and said, "This is the Oregon Trail. Here is the Fort Hall. When they reach Fort Hall the people who are for Oregon will keep on this trail going northwest. Those for California will turn here at Fort Hall and go southwest, going down the Humboldt River. This straight line going west from Little Sandy passes south of Salt Lake and joins somewhere along here."

"Then it is shorter," said Eleanor. "Are you really going to start a school for girls? My father always said girls didn't need an education. I went a little while, and I learned to read. Then he made me stay home. I never studied geography. I wish I had some books to read."

"I'll lend you some. How about *Pride and Prejudice*?"

Mrs. Breen, who was trying to corral her three youngest boys, said flatly to Eleanor, "Girls don't need to learn to read books. A few letters and some numbers are all they need to know. I learned the catechism by heart and all the Hail Marys. Mr. Breen can read and write. He learned in Ireland when he was a boy."

She then turned to Tamsen and said scornfully, "School learning makes feminists out of girls. Mr. Breen says you are a writer. The men said you sent some writings to the *Springfield Journal*. They said you gave it to that scout who was going east, the one we met before we were at Fort Laramie. Mr. Breen says that Ann Royall was a feminist. She was a writer. It was indecent the way she sneaked up on the president while he was bathing.

"I haven't heard in years people call anyone an Ann Royall. You see she is a publisher in Washington. Once when she was a young reporter she wanted to interview President Adams. He refused her. The president often went down to the Potomac about five in the morning for a quick dip in the buff. So one morning Ann Royall sat down on his clothes and refused to leave until he granted the interview. I am not a reporter. I write poems and articles about flowers. Mr. Francis of the *Springfield Journal* said he would print anything I write about our experiences on this trip. I keep a diary."

"So does Mr. Breen. Well, I better get back to my wagon. Isabelle will be waking up from her nap."

"My Peggy is a year old. Your little girl is about the same age, isn't she? Peggy has been napping, too," said Eleanor.

Mrs. Breen left pushing her three little boys ahead of her. Tamsen's little girls stood beside her. Now they walked to the wagon and she lifted them in. She asked Frances to hand her one of the books lying on a box. It was *Pride and Prejudice*.

Eleanor opened the book and happily leafed through it. Tamsen saw Virginia Reed on her pony and motioned her over. Leanna and Elitha, also on horses, came with Virginia. The three girls praised the book to Eleanor.

Tamsen asked, "How is your mother? Does she still have that migraine headache?"

"It seemed to get better this morning as soon as we

left South Pass and were coming down. Papa wondered if the headache was caused by the altitude. Now that we are lower they may get better. She was even hungry this morning."

"I wish I had time to go see her now, but the men want us to get on the move."

"Papa said we could ride horseback a little while, if we stay in sight of the wagons," said Leanna. Then apparently catching sight of the book in Eleanor's hands, she added, "I like that book. I just finished reading it."

Eleanor looked up from her book, then glanced up the trail that came down from South Pass.

"Look, Mrs. Donner. There are some more wagons coming down the trail. There are four wagons. It must be two outfits. The first one is just one wagon and hardly any stock. There are three wagons in the second outfit and more stock. They are not moving very fast."

Tamsen watched the approaching emigrants, then said, "I suppose they will be going by the Fort Hall trail. A better choice than ours."

Then putting her arms around the younger woman, she said, "They are ready to leave now. Eleanor dear, a woman must let her man follow his heart and her heart must go with him."

Chapter 2

After leaving Little Sandy the newly formed party of seventy-five people and twenty wagons accompanied by a herd of horses, spare oxen, loose cattle, and dogs followed the desert trail of granite sand southwesterly toward Fort Bridger.

George's outfit was in the lead. He had three covered wagons, each drawn by two yoke of oxen.

"Gee! Haw!" he called and cracked his whip over the oxen. They were placid creatures, and he did not touch them with the whip. Its noise and his voice were their signal to move until an equally sonorous whoa brought them to a halt. Behind him his two hired teamsters brought his baggage wagons into line.

Tamsen and the five girls rode in the family wagon. George walked beside it. Tamsen rode on the front seat and sometimes the girls rode with her, but more often they liked to watch from the back, peeking out from behind the canvas curtains. Their favorite saddle horses were tethered to the wagon.

James Reed's three wagons were in the rear of the party and his three teamsters were in charge of the wagons. Milt Elliott, a long-time friend of Reed, was more skilled than James Smith or Walter Herron, so he was in charge of the Pioneer Palace Car. He drove three span of oxen.

James Reed himself, with his stepdaughter Virginia on her pony Billie, rode ahead of the party on his mare, Glaucus. He scouted to find a good camping place.

Tamsen was still depressed. She had accepted his choice of this cutoff without enthusiasm and had not yet returned to her usual buoyancy and cheerfulness. She usually had busy hands, knitting or writing in her diary. Today her hands lay idle in her lap except when automatically she reached out to pull Georgia's and Eliza's sunbonnets up to shade their faces. Frances had joined Leanna and Elitha at the back.

Even conversation with George or the girls seemed to dry up. Then the heat seemed to melt her mood into a dull apathy.

James Reed and Virginia returned with their report.

Reed said, "There are some rough spots ahead, but I found a good camping place beside a river. I think it must be the Big Sandy, but it's not so big this time of year. We can easily drive across. There are signs of campers."

"I suppose they have grazed out all of the good grass," said Jake Donner, coming forward to hear the report.

"Not too bad," said Reed. "They must have gone upstream for grazing. It looks as if there is plenty of grass downstream. Campers have made fire rings, and there is wood lying around. It must have been a good-sized party, or possibly two parties. Some of them might be only a couple of days ahead of us."

"I know Harlan's party was planning on taking this route," said George. "When we got Hastings's letter back on Sweetwater Creek, Harlan said he would go and meet Lansford Hastings at Fort Bridger."

"And the Young party, too," said Reed.

"Yes," said George complacently, "Hastings is waiting for us at Fort Bridger."

Tamsen's spirit lightened. In her serenity she took up her knitting.

Charles Stanton, on horseback, joined the men. Stanton had been a prosperous merchant in Chicago and after some financial reverses had moved to Springfield. He had attended the book club which met in George's home. Tamsen was reading Emerson's Essays to the group, and

Stanton had been a welcome addition to the club for he participated in the discussions.

Last year Tamsen had read Lansford Hastings's book. That was the book that caused all these people to take this shortcut.

Though Stanton rode his own horse, his baggage was in George's supply wagon.

Stanton asked Reed, "Any chance of game?"

"No big game. Maybe some rabbits. I think I saw a sage hen with her brood scurrying out into the sagebrush. I think you might find some game along the river."

John Denton rode up on horseback and said, "If you are going hunting I'd like to go along."

"That's a true Englishman for you," said George. "His friends are going with Boggs, so Reed said he could put his baggage in the Reed supply wagon."

The horsemen gradually outdistanced the plodding oxen.

The heat made Tamsen drowsy. She stopped knitting, and the garment lay motionless in her lap. Her thoughts lazily flowed in a fantasy. She was a school mistress --a school set in a garden-- always green-- young ladies strolling-- easels set up among the flowers-- color.

Then with a start came reality. Color. The sun was low in the west. The whole sky seemed golden. Tamsen turned and called to her girls, "Come here and look at the sunset!"

The girls scrambled to the front of the wagon.

Splashes of orange, red, and gold deepened across the wide expanse of the sky, silhouetting the distant mountains like a purple city of spires and cathedrals. The beauty seemed to envelope the world, to pavilion it. Tamsen thought of her paint supplies. She wondered if she could one capture this color? Maybe. But no one could catch that feeling of a magic world beyond.

The trail sloped to the river and soon they were at the campsite. Quickly they gathered fuel for the campfires.

Tamsen and Elizabeth brought cheese, pickles, dried fruit, tea, and coffee from their supply wagons. Stanton brought them two rabbits and a sage hen.

George and Jake milked their cows, and the teamsters drove them down to pasture.

Noah James came to George. He was leading a horse. "Mr. Donner," he said, "The man who has been riding in the covered wagon asked me to take this horse to pasture. I think he must be sick."

"That's Luke Halloran," said George. "I told him he could ride with us. He put his baggage in our wagon."

"Luke Halloran? Who is he?" asked Tamsen.

"He was with the Cartwrights, but they went by Fort Hall," he said. He sounded confident that any sane man would prefer traveling by the cutoff.

"I'll go see him," said Tamsen

As soon as she saw him she realized he was quite ill. In this wagon there were the sacks of grass the men had cut to use when pasturage was scarce. Tamsen pummeled the bags to flatten them, put a blanket over them, and made Luke comfortable.

In seeking for a suitable blanket she had hunted in a pile of extras packed in a canvas bag. In that bag was a special patchwork quilt she had made from scraps of her girls' dresses. Under the neatly sewed patches were bills in the amount of ten thousand dollars. Only the family and James Reed knew of this quilt. Taking out a more suitable blanket and tucking the quilt at the bottom of the bag, she made Luke comfortable.

Chapter 3

The next day the emigrants got an early start to enjoy the cool morning before the heat of noon. The trail continued on gravelly sand, over boulders, up and down hillocks, and across streams that were now low in the summer heat and easy to ford.

They camped earlier than the day before. Here was a stream and ample pasturage. Here was a chance for more cooking, and preparation of food that took a longer time: hominy with salt pork and beans.

After supper Tamsen carried some food to Luke Halloran. "Here is some chicken broth," she said, laughing. "Of course, not your usual chicken. Stanton got a number of sage hens this afternoon."

Luke smiled and expressed his thanks.

He looks so gaunt, thought Tamsen. Then she noticed some bottles of medicine by his pillow. "Are you taking this medicine?"

"Yes. That's something Edwin Bryant gave me. I never took that kind before. It's homeopathic."

"I know Edwin Bryant," said Tamsen. "He studied homeopathy for a while. Later in St. Louis he published a newspaper."

"Yes, I talked with him quite a bit. He had medicines left over from his student days. He gave them to me and some to Mrs. Thornton."

"I think he liked newspaper work better than being a doctor. He said he was going to write about what he saw in California. You know, at Laramie he sold his oxen and wagon and joined the horseback riders. One of our teamsters, Hiram Miller, did the same thing. He quit our outfit, bought a horse, and is riding to California with Mr. Bryant," said Tamsen.

"Oh, Hiram Miller is one of your friends? I wanted to join the horsemen, too, and get to California quicker. But Edwin Bryant thought I was too sick. He gave me these pills to supply me until I get to California," Luke said.

His head drooped on the pillow. Then with a start he sat up and asked, "What's that? A fiddle? Is Ann Eliza Fowler in this party? She used to play when we were on the prairie. We sang songs and danced and jigged to Irish tunes. It was lots fun. Frank Kellog played the fiddle, too. I think he stayed with Governor Boggs's party."

"I think the Fowlers are in the Harlan party, and George says they must be at Fort Bridger by this time. But you lie down and rest. I'll go see who is playing."

Joining George, Tamsen asked, "Who's that man playing the fiddle?"

"Patrick Dolan. Everybody calls him Uncle Patrick. He is a friend of the Breens. I don't think he is related. He comes from Iowa but was born in Ireland."

"Are the Breens the ones with all those little boys?"

"Yes, six boys and a baby girl. Breen was also born in Ireland. He seems to be quite prosperous. He has three wagons and a lot of stock."

"Play us that new tune, Uncle Patrick," said one of the Breen boys, as he began prancing and singing, "Oh Susannah." By the time he got to, "With my banjo on my knee," a dozen boys were cavorting around. Young men were hurriedly coming from their peacefully grazing stock, and young women were hastily finishing their tasks around the campfire.

Uncle Patrick switched to other popular tunes. Many began to dance. Patrick Breen danced an Irish jig.

"I know only a few of these people," said Tamsen. "Of course, we know the Eddys. I see him, but not

Eleanor. She probably has her two little ones asleep. They love dancing. Who are those other dancing couples?"

"Mrs. Murphy's family. Do you know there are thirteen of them? Two of her daughters are married. There are three grandchildren, two sons-in-law and five younger children. I don't know the girls apart, yet, but I think Stanton is dancing with the unmarried one. How about you, Tamsen? Would you like to give it a whirl?" George said.

"It's hardly a dance floor, being sand and gravel."

"Old folks like us don't go dancing," said Jake Donner. "You don't see James Reed out there promenading around, either. He is a younger man than you are."

"The reason the Reeds are not out there dancing," said Tamsen, "is that Margaret is ill. She has terrible migraine headaches. Oh, look! Who is that?"

The dancers, too, had stopped to watch. Patrick paused a moment, and then started playing a waltz.

"That's Mr. Wolfinger," said George.

Wolfinger was helping his wife out of their wagon as she climbed over the wheel. Mrs. Wolfinger had on a dress of velvet and satin. The neckline of lace ruching spread out over her shoulders and dipped into a *V*. She wore a gold chain that sparkled with a jeweled emblem. On her arms and in her hair was more jewelry. She walked over on uneven ground and tested the dancing area with her slipper. Startled, she withdrew from the gravelly area.

Patrick fiddled a rollicking tune. The dancers began again, laughing and shouting. Each couple took a turn for a close look at Mrs. Wolfinger's clothes and jewelry.

"Does she know those young people are laughing at her?" asked Tamsen.

"I imagine she does," said George. "She has spunk."

Wolfinger stood by his wife courteously until all the dancers dispersed.

Chapter 4

The following day was much the same. They camped on Black Fork Creek.

While Elizabeth and Tamsen prepared their meal they shared tidbits of news. Elizabeth was Aunt Betsy to all the young children, and their mothers turned to Elizabeth for advice and to share confidences and gossip.

Elizabeth said, "The young women were making fun of Mrs. Wolfinger wearing all those fancy clothes. I think they are just jealous, especially of her fine jewelry. I'm pretty sure it's real."

"George says that the Wolfingers are from Germany. Probably she is not used to country dances. She was dressed for a ballroom dance," said Tamsen.

"Maybe you're right. She isn't very friendly. Maybe it's because she can't speak English," said George.

"She speaks it correctly, but like someone who has studied it but not used it much. I heard her speaking German to her husband."

"Do you understand German?" asked Elizabeth.

"I understand only a few words. I studied French at the academy in North Carolina."

"French? Why would anybody want to study French?"

"Oh, perhaps to read French novels," said Tamsen laughing.

Elizabeth looked puzzled, then asked, "Studied? Didn't you teach there?"

"Yes, I did. At first I taught the younger children. I also went on with my studies: botany, French, and painting. Later I taught botany right there in the academy."

"Why did you quit teaching there?"

"I married and so was not allowed to teach."

"But they allowed you to teach at Sugar Creek."

"I was a widow by that time. School boards seem to like to hire widows."

Seemingly by mutual consent they changed the subject. Both were reticent and they did not talk about their first marriages. Tamsen was unwilling to share her feeling about that unhappy fortnight when her husband and two small children died in the epidemic. Elizabeth's first marriage was well known. Her two boys of that marriage still carried their father's name, Hook.

"You were teaching botany in the Sugar Creek school when George met you," said Elizabeth, stating a fact which everybody knew.

"Yes, I was actually trespassing on George's land. I was taking my class out on a trip exploring for plant specimens. He teases me and says that he is the specimen I found."

Tamsen took a plate of food to Luke Halloran. He seemed better, more aware and ready to talk.

"You have a box labeled school supplies. Are you a schoolteacher?" he asked.

"Yes, I am going to start a school for young ladies in California."

"You have had schooling? Of course, a lady like you would have. My sister wanted to have some schooling but my father said girls did not need it. It makes feminists out of them. He wanted me to go to college, but I had to quit on account of my health. I am sure that I will get well in California. Will you please ask Charles Stanton to ride my mare part of the time? That would spell his horse and exercise mine."

Tamsen promised to deliver the message and then left. She went to her other wagon to prepare the sleeping rolls for her three little girls.

She found the girls, along with the small children in the camp, scampering about. Elizabeth was still at the campfire preparing food for a quick breakfast. Elizabeth had sent her seven-year-old Mary to join Mrs. Breen and Tamsen in rounding up the small children.

Mrs. Breen said firmly, "You boys may watch from the back of the wagon. I don't want you underfoot when the ladies are dancing."

"Same for you," said Tamsen to her girls.

"Can I watch with Mary? We won't get in the way of the dancers," said Frances. "Mary is seven years old and I'm going to have a birthday and I'll be seven, too. Can I?"

"May I," corrected Tamsen.

"May I go with Mary," said Frances dutifully.

George joined them and said, "Well, Little Professor, there's no vacation for schoolteachers. Seems our little pupil took one. Everybody is gathering for the larking. Well, not everybody. Those Dutchmen over there are hanging back."

"Dutchmen?"

"Jake calls them that. But they are from Germany, except Hardkoop, who was born in Belgium."

"Weren't the Wolfingers born in Germany?" asked Tamsen. "Oh, there she is standing by their wagon. She's not wearing her fancy ballroom dress or jewelry. Look at the Kesebergs? My, he is a handsome man, tall and blond. There, Mr. Reed is talking to him."

As George and Tamsen got closer they heard James Reed say angrily, "You're a brute. There will be no wife beating in this outfit. If this happens again out you go."

Tamsen could hear Phillipine Keseberg with her two crying children in the back of their covered wagon. Her shocked thought was that indeed he was a brute.

Speaking in a low voice to George, Tamsen said, "Look at his eyes. They are black pools of hate."

Tamsen well knew why Keseberg hated Reed. Reed had been the leader of the men who had kicked Keseberg out of the party back on the plains when he robbed an Indian grave. George had persuaded the men to let Keseberg back into the party because of his wife and children.

"Well, I think I'll go over to see if Margaret Reed is well enough to come out and watch the dancing," said Tamsen. "I see Virginia is already out there, watching with Leanna and Elitha."

"Yes," said George. "They will soon be joining in the square dances. I want to have a good whirl with you tonight, but I want to talk with Reed now."

Margaret said, "Yes, I'm so much better. Patti and I are coming out."

The next morning they were on the trail early, hoping to reach Fort Bridger by afternoon.

Usually at some hour every day Tamsen wrote in her diary, which she kept in the ample pocket of her skirt. This morning she checked over her diary. There were some interesting happenings since she had sent some items to the *Springfield Journal* last June. She wondered if there would be a chance to send anything back to the *Springfield Journal*. She leaned over the wheel and asked George his opinion.

"Oh, go ahead and write the news. We'll leave the letter at Fort Bridger. Someone might be going east."

They came in sight of Fort Bridger at noon of July 28.

Chapter 5

Fort Bridger was not really a fort, but a trading post. There were two log cabins, a horse corral, and a blacksmith shop. Several streams meandered around in a wide arc and then came together in the Black Fork River.

The families scattered each into the most advantageous spot for pasturing their stock and for building their fires.

Leaving their teamsters and Jake's older boys to care for the stock, George and Jake Donner and James Reed went to the shops to find Lansford Hastings and Jim Bridger.

Neither man seemed to be around. They met drifters, scouts, and trappers. There was loud talking and much swearing. Bridger was expected to bring a load of supplies from some trading post down Santa Fe way. For many years Bridger had been a trapper and was on good terms with the Indians. When he took the skins to a trading post he would return with supplies for himself and enough to trade with the Indians. Until two years ago the Oregon Trail had passed through Fort Bridger.

The men milling around the shops and corral said they danged sure hoped Bridger would get in before nightfall and bring plenty of whiskey and ammunition.

George and James Reed asked about Lansford Hastings.

"He left here a week ago with the Harlan and Young parties. They had sixty-six wagons," said one man. "Hastings didn't know that any more parties were coming. But sixty-six wagons will make a hell of a trail. They'll have to build some of it themselves. That'll make it easy for you folks to follow."

George carried the news to Tamsen.

She said, "Then we should get on the road bright and early tomorrow morning, The women can be ready. They have done their washing. There are a number of pools along the river's edge. Things will be dry soon and we can take them in."

George said, "We can't leave tomorrow. We ought to set our tires and there is a good blacksmith shop here. Also the grass is good, fine grazing for the stock. By the way, I hired a man to take Hiram Miller's place. He seemed a likable little monkey. His name is Jean Baptiste Trudeau."

"French?" asked Tamsen.

"He is a crossbreed with French, Indian, and Mexican ancestry. He claims he can do anything. I don't know how far you can trust him but we do need a teamster badly."

"Yes, we do. Still I can't blame Hiram Miller who left us to get to California quicker by horseback."

"Tamsen, keep the girls away from the shops and corral. There is just too much going on."

Just then Bridger and his partner Vasquez, spurring their mules for a last dash, arrived to the shouts of the men.

Bridger quickly unpacked his liquor. The bottles were snatched and the drinking began. The Dutchmen of the Donner party took their bottles over to their wagons and had their drinks. The Indians, who had stood quietly apart from the other men all afternoon now joined the buyers. They went over to the shelter of a pile of old lumber that had been used as a stockade when the place was really a fort. They soon were dead drunk and stretched out on the boards.

James Reed said to George and Jake Donner, "It's disgusting. Bad whiskey. Let's go over to my wagon, and

I'll bring out some decent stuff. Better bring our teamsters, too. They got work to do tomorrow, and we don't want drunks. We got to get our wagons in top shape."

"I hired a new teamster this afternoon. He's a kind of desert waif," said George with a grin. "I bet he never tasted anything like your stuff. We have Sam Carpenter and Noah James. John Denton has gone hunting with Charles Stanton and William Eddy. Down the river there are trees. It looks like a likely place for hunting."

"Bridger says there is no big game around here. There may be some in the Wasatch mountains," said Reed.

The next day was a busy one for the men. Most of them were working around the shops. A few men, besides the trio of Eddy, Stanton, and Denton, went hunting. The older boys tended the stock. Virginia, Elitha, and Leanna went horseback riding. The women prepared food. Bread was to be baked, and cornmeal mush was prepared, ready to be sliced when cold. It could then be fried lightly and served with honey.

A scream reached the ears of every man working in the shops and all the women at their tasks.

"Mamma! Mamma!" the scream continued.

"Holy Saints, it's my Eddie," said Patrick Breen.

Breen, Bridger, and George got to the boy first. He was lying on the ground in front of the horse corral with an unsaddled horse beside him.

Between sobs, Eddie said, "I know how to ride without a saddle."

Bridger said, "He didn't throw you. He must have stumbled. Hey, boy. Your trouser leg is all soaked with blood." He dashed to his tool shed and returned with a long knife. He snatched a blanket from a pile in the corral. He slit the trouser leg and exposed a bleeding gash in the leg. He stanched the bleeding with a blanket.

"I want Mamma," said Eddie between sobs.

Breen kept repeating, "You should have stayed with Jonnie and helped watch the stock. Don't cry now. Be a big boy. The saints bless us."

Every mother who heard Eddie's cries knew its timbre, and every small child sought its mother. Mrs. Breen was the first to arrive and Tamsen was just behind her. When Tamsen saw the blood-soaked blanket she was horrified. Telling George to get a bucket of water, she dashed back to the wagon and grabbed a handful of clean muslin strips, the kind they used to strain milk. She also took her medicine kit.

Mrs. Breen said to her husband, "Go on to the wagon. Isabelle is all alone. Light a candle to Saint Joseph. I'll fix Eddie's leg. The saints bless us."

When Tamsen returned she saw that Mrs. Breen had already unwrapped the dirty blanket from Eddie's leg. She was arguing with Bridger who was holding a long sharp knife.

"You will not cut his leg off. I won't have it."

"But, lady, it will have to be cut off. The leg is broken."

"I won't have it. Mr. Donner, get me some wood. I see lots of it. Over there where those Indians are is a big pile of wood."

Tamsen handed the clean cloths to Mrs. Breen who kept sponging the wound while Bridger kept arguing and flourishing his knife. Tamsen handed Mrs. Breen a bottle of turpentine. Eddie winced when his mother sponged his wound with it.

"You're a big boy," said Mrs. Breen.

Tamsen gave Eddie sips of paregoric. Mrs. Breen was shocked. She said, "That's baby medicine."

"Yes I know, but it has opium and it will deaden the pain."

Eddie relaxed and his mother straightened his leg. She took the splints that George cut for her and the cloth that Tamsen had brought and bandaged it.

Bridger, unconvinced, shook his head and kept repeating, "Infection will set in. It will swell up and he will die."

George carried the boy to the Breen wagon.

Chapter 6

The next day, Wednesday July 29, the women expected that the party would be moving on by early afternoon, so their household chores were done. George announced it would be another day before they would get going because more wagon repairs needed to be made.

James Reed said, "When I was in the business of building furniture I hired Milt Elliot and Walter Heron. They are quite knowledgeable about building, but even they don't know too much about working around a forge. They are good teamsters, however."

"That's like our teamsters," said George. "Only John Denton has had any experience working with metals. He came from England two years ago, where he was a gunsmith."

"There's work to do. I'd better get on their tails. We want to get on the road," said Jake.

"There's space to work now," said George. "The others around here have their whiskey, ammunition, and other supplies packed on their mules and are about to leave. Now our men can get the tools and into the blacksmith shops. Well, by jingo! It looks as if someone else is joining us."

Tamsen, who had been standing with the men, quickly turned her head at George's exclamation. She said, "Mrs. Eddy and I saw that outfit coming down from South Pass just as we were leaving Little Sandy. I presumed that they would be following Governor Boggs. To have waited for them there would have delayed you."

George looked at her keenly, then said cheerfully, "This route is working out fine."

Their conversation was interrupted as the driver of the covered wagon urged his oxen on. William

McCutchen, his wife Amanda, and his one-year-old Harriet were now members of the Donner party.

McCutchen was a big man, over six feet tall, and broad shouldered. Harriet was enthusiastically received by the children.

McCutchen was also welcomed by the men. He seemed to know more about how one tightened iron tires on wooden wheels. He was always ready to help the others.

It was soon nap time for the younger children. Tamsen allowed her stepdaughters to go horseback riding with Mary Murphy and Virginia. She was about to write a few things in her diary. The children's nap time was her usual time for that.

As she wrote down the date, July 29, she was startled when she realized that two months ago today was the day Margaret Reed's mother died. She decided she must go now and visit Margaret. As she passed Elizabeth Donner's wagon she heard Mary Donner arguing with her mother that she didn't need a nap. She was going to be eight years old. Only her little brothers needed a nap.

She passed the Breen's cabin. The little ones were probably asleep. Eddie was arguing with his mother that he could walk on his leg now, but his mother was not going to let him use it so soon after his accident.

The next wagon belonged to Mrs. Murphy. Tamsen did not know much about her, except that her daughter Mary was Leanna's age and that her two older daughters were married. The sons-in-law were the teamsters for the two wagons. The next wagon was the Reeds's. This was the special wagon that he had built in his furniture-making shop. Instead of climbing over a wheel, Tamsen knocked on a door at the side.

Margaret opened the door and Tamsen entered a

small room furnished with a couch and spring seats. The wagon had been made wide by extending planking out over the wheels. There were two stories. On the higher level were the beds and on the lower level were compartments for storage. There was a sheet-iron stove with the pipe going up through the canvas top.

Margaret greeted Tamsen happily. Tamsen had often ridden in this little room when Mrs. Keyes was still alive. She had insisted on accompanying Margaret to California, and it was in this room she spent her days and nights from April 26 to May 29. She now lay in a grave in Kansas.

"You do look better," said Tamsen in greeting.

"Yes, I have been fine ever since we got over the pass. Do you realize that it is two months since mother passed away?"

Tamsen nodded. She noted that eight-year-old Patti was seated on the couch that had been her grandmother's bed, the couch that James Reed had especially constructed for Mrs. Keyes's comfort.

Margaret said with a sigh, "Patti misses her grandmother so much. She insists on sleeping on that couch every night and she sits all day on it cuddling that doll my mother made for her. Patti dear, you should take a nap. Tommy and Junior are already asleep."

Patti lay back on the couch and closed her eyes.

Margaret and Tamsen were soon in conversation, ignoring whether Patti was awake or asleep. Margaret said, "My mother was so thrilled to learn that you are planning to start a young ladies' finishing school in California. She was always concerned about Virginia's and Patti's education."

"I'm thrilled, too. I have dreamed of it a long time, even before I met George. But you know, among the farmers' families they don't think that girls need an education. Did you go to a finishing school?" asked Tamsen.

"Oh, yes. I was married to Mr. Bachenstoe right after I finished. I was nineteen. I think mother thought education important because it meant a better chance to marry well. Anyway it seemed that way when I married Mr. Bachenstoe."

"I noticed," said Tamsen, "that she always called Virginia by her full name, Virginia Bachenstoe."

"Yes, the Bachenstoes are high society. She didn't want Virginia to forget it. Mr. Bachenstoe was quite a bit older than I, but my mother felt he was suitable. After he died, Virginia and I went to live with mother."

"How did your mother feel about Mr. Reed?"

"I met him through some of my friends. It took some time to persuade my mother that he was high enough society. You know Reed is really Reedowski. His family are of Polish nobility. They left Poland because of a political upheaval and went to Ireland. That's where Mr. Reed grew up. Then he came to this country. He served in the Black Hawk Indian campaign under Abe Lincoln. At first my mother did not approve. When he had success in business she gave in for me to marry him. Yet she always felt she must remind everybody that he descended from nobility."

"You can't guess what I was called yesterday: a feminist."

"Really? Teaching is hardly a man's world."

"No. But writing for a newspaper is. I guess everybody knows that I sent an account of our experiences to the *Springfield Journal*. Mr. Francis promised to print anything I send. I have some more ready, but I don't think we will be meeting any scouts going east while on this cutoff trail. I have also written poetry, but now I am most interested in writing the book about the flowers of the West. I have preserved specimens on this trip, but I have not had time to paint the pictures. Anyway, I have the flower collection and can paint the pictures accurately."

"How could anybody think painting the picture of flowers was feminist. To me a feminist is one who lectures and campaigns like Susan B. Anthony and Elizabeth Cady Stanton. They lecture and campaign for women's rights, women's suffrage, the right to own property, and for abolition."

"I guess we don't qualify as feminists, not in actions, but I do believe in their goals," said Tamsen.

That evening George told Tamsen it would be another day before the men were ready to leave.

"Another day's delay!" said Tamsen. "I really should call on Mrs. Murphy. Mrs. Keseberg seems to avoid me, probably because I overheard the conversation with Mr. Reed about her husband beating her. She seems to be friendly with the young mothers whose children play with her little girl. Mrs. Wolfinger is so noncommittal we do little more than exchange greetings."

Tamsen called on Mrs. Murphy. Her two married daughters, Sarah Foster and Harriet Pike, had gone to the river to do some washing and had left three little children in Mrs. Murphy's care.

Mrs. Murphy said, "No, Mary, you may not go horseback riding with the Donner girls. I need you to look after these little wild Indians. Luckily my own three boys are out from under foot now. They are down at the shops with my son-in-law. Harriet is so fussy about her little girls' clothes. It seems to me that every day is wash day. The children can surely find the dirt."

Tamsen realized Mrs. Murphy was taking out her

irritation in talking. One question about where her home had been was enough to keep Mrs. Murphy talking.

"We are from Tennessee really, but I went to Missouri after my husband died. I had a chance to run a boardinghouse. Most of the boarders were men. Women don't board out unless they are schoolteachers. It's easy for pretty girls to get married with so many young men around. My sons-in-law are both named William, so I use their other names, Foster and Pike."

That evening Tamsen told George she had visited the Murphys, and she added, "I got an earful."

Early on the morning of Friday, July 30, they left Fort Bridger.

Chapter 7

The party left Fort Bridger early. Some of the women had not yet finished their morning chores. Eliza Williams, the maid who had been in Margaret Reed's household for years, had to finish her preparation of milk for churning while on the road. That was easy for her because Reed had constructed an area in the wagon for her to perform her household tasks.

The mothers of the small children were still busy with their dressing and feeding.

Tamsen had barely settled herself on the seat of the wagon and was about to pick up her knitting when she realized that George had brought his oxen to a halt. Then she saw Charles Stanton and James Reed who had earlier ridden on ahead. Tamsen climbed out and George joined the men. Jake Donner and William and Eleanor Eddy also joined them. Stanton and Reed had dismounted.

"Look at that trail going north," said Stanton as he took a map from his saddle pack. "Oh, I see. These marks are part of the old Oregon Trail. They told us at the fort that, until two years ago, the trail to Oregon came through Fort Bridger and then turned north to Fort Hall. That's why Jim Bridger established a trading post at the nearest watering place, there on the Black Fork. The present trail is a shortcut to Little Sandy and South Pass."

"Why did all the trails have to go over South Pass?" asked Eddy. "Surely there are more places where a person could cross the continental divide."

Everybody turned to Charles Stanton. They knew of his interest in geology and maps. They respected him and often sought his opinion.

Stanton said, "A few years ago the government set up a commission to have surveys made of the various routes that the scouts had explored. The commission hired the surveyor Charles Frémont for the job. He made such a good map that the government ordered a thousand at the first printing. So this route soon became the popular one."

John Denton asked, "Is that the same Frémont who is now fighting in California?"

"Yes. At Fort Laramie I heard that Frémont had formed a company of volunteers to fight the Mexicans. I think that most of those that went ahead on horseback were planning to join Frémont."

"Let's get back to our wagons and get going. We can't dilly-dally around here all day," said Jake Donner.

The company moved. First there was a stretch of sandy desert, then narrow ravines. They went up over high ridges, then down into narrow canyons. The second day there were more ridges, and finally a canyon with a wide spot for pasturage.

Elizabeth's boy Solomon went scouting while the men pitched camp. He came running back, waving a piece of paper.

He shouted, "Mr. Hastings left this paper fastened to a bush."

He handed it to his stepfather who said, "You go get your Aunt Tamsen to read this."

Tamsen studied the weather-beaten slip of paper while the men gathered around.

Finally she said, "Hastings calls this place Weber Canyon. He says the trail is bad and he is afraid his own party can't get through. He says that if we need help he will come back and guide us by a better and shorter route."

"How did Hastings know we were coming by the cutoff?" asked Stanton.

"I told Harlan at Sweetwater. He was always a jump ahead," said Eddy.

George said, "I'll bet Harlan gave Hastings a push to move on."

"Why did he take his party down this canyon if it is so bad? You can see their trail there. He is supposed to have explored it and should have known," protested Jake.

George said, "Back at Fort Bridger they admitted that nobody explored this with a wagon. Hastings and the others have gone this way only on horseback."

"Any fool knows that horses can go on trails that oxen can't," said Jake.

"I guess he found that out with his Harlan-Young bunch," said another.

Tamsen, for the first time, had a grudging respect for Lansford Hastings, and she said, "He didn't even know that we would be coming and still he came back on a horse when he found that his wagons were having trouble."

James Reed said decisively, "I'll ride ahead and overtake him. I'll ask him to come back and guide us."

George said, "Maybe a couple of men should go with you."

Charlès Stanton and William McCutchen volunteered. McCutchen, six feet six inches tall, swung on a horse borrowed from George. Slender Charles Stanton agilely sprang up on his own horse. Reed rode one of his heavier horses, leaving Glaucus, his racing mare, in camp. The three riders started down the trail that Hastings had declared too hazardous for wagons.

Chapter 8

The next four days the company waited in camp. The Breens, the Donners, and the hired men who worked for James Reed spent time with their stock. They cut grass and stacked it for use when it would not be so plentiful. Stanton, Denton, and Eddy went hunting.

Back at the fort the women got so well acquainted that they mingled socially. Gossip and household chores went hand in hand. There was always bread to be baked, hominy and beans to be cooked, and clothes to be washed in the stream.

The young mothers took their children out to the grassy areas to play and joined Tamsen in looking for plants.

Elizabeth Donner made cookies. The children were fascinated watching her bake them over the campfire. Soon Elizabeth became the confidante of the mothers.

Leanna and Elitha joined Virginia in looking after the younger children. While the little ones napped, Tamsen and Margaret allowed them to go horseback riding.

Elizabeth said to Tamsen, "The women are concerned about Phillipine Keseberg. They heard noises in the Keseberg wagon. Now that Mr. Reed is gone they don't trust Keseberg. They wish you would ask George to talk to him."

Tamsen reported the conversation to George. He sauntered over to Lewis Keseberg and they talked quite a while. When George returned he said, "He is burning with hatred toward Reed. I just let him spout off. Then we talked about this and that. He is an interesting talker. I told him, sort of offhand, that in America wife beating was looked down on. I think you've heard of the end of that caper."

When alone with Elizabeth, Tamsen said, "Marriage is different on different levels of society as well as in different parts of the world."

"Like Keseberg thinking it was his right to beat his wife?" asked Elizabeth.

"Yes, and other differences. In North Carolina a girl went to finishing school so that she could make a good marriage. I am not referring to the aristocracy with slaves, but average middle-class families are very conscious of class and mothers scheme to get their daughters suitable husbands. The wife has to maintain the husband's status. In turn the husband takes care of the wife. The mothers say love will come later, after they are married. Also it was the custom for the husband to make all the decisions."

"Like James" Reed and Margaret," said Elizabeth.

"Yes. Of course, you know that Mr. Reed is a descendant of Polish aristocracy. His attitude toward women reflects old world attitudes. It seems to me the younger women, Amanda McCuthchen, Eleanor Eddy, and Mrs. Murphy's two married daughters are more like partners with their husbands."

"Jake says that the men call William and Eleanor Eddy lovey-doveys. They are still at the romantic stage," said Elizabeth.

Tamsen looked quickly at Elizabeth and wondered if she divided the romantic stage from mature marriage. Elizabeth's first marriage had been to Mr. Hook and she had borne William and Solomon. Jake was the father of her five younger children. The Hook boys were a great help to him. A partnership of interest--was that what Elizabeth meant by mature marriage? Tamsen too, was a widow when she met George.

A feeling of sadness came over her with the memory. Her own two babies lay beside their father in the grave. After Mr. Dozier's death she had returned to her friends in Massachusetts. Her father had died and her stepmother had remarried. Her brother had moved out to Illinois. She joined him and taught in nearby Auburn. The next year she taught in Sugar Creek where there were older and more advanced pupils. She met George when she took her botany class on a field trip.

She sensed the approval of her friends. Hers was a good marriage, a suitable one, suitable for George as he had two small daughters to raise, and suitable for her, for married women had a better place in the community than a spinster or widow. Tamsen knew that in this marriage she had found something more than just status, something special not always found in second marriages.

Elizabeth and Tamsen both knew the statistical facts of the other's marriage, but they never discussed the subject.

Three days passed, and the riders had not yet returned. Tamsen realized that George was beginning to worry, and in true wifely fashion she began to reassure him, hiding her own worry.

The tension among the men exploded into arguing, quarreling, shouting, and cursing. George tried to calm their worries, but was only half successful. Their anger was directed against both Lansford Hastings and James Reed.

Margaret Reed and Amanda McCutchen were worried about their husbands running out of food.

Tamsen reassured them, "They have their guns and will probably find some game. Stanton is a good botanist and he should be able to recognize edibles."

About noon on August 11, Virginia, who had been riding her pony, came dashing to the family wagon calling, "Mama. Mama. I saw a man on horseback down the trail.

I think it's Papa. I'm going to meet him."

The word spread, and with cheers, everybody ran to the Reed wagon.

Soon James Reed and Virginia appeared, and Patti Reed said, "That isn't Papa's horse."

Tamsen asked anxiously, "Where are Stanton and McCutchen?"

"They will be along soon," said Reed. "All three of our horses gave out. I got this one from the Harlan-Young camp, but Stanton and McCutchen are waiting until their own horses are ready. We won't wait for them but get right on the trail."

"Did you find Lansford Hastings?" asked George.

"Yes, I did. He's leading the Harlan-Young party. They were camped by the south shore of Salt Lake."

"Hastings promised to come back with you and lead us. At least that is what he wrote on the note he left on the stick," said Tamsen.

"He ought to be good as his word," said Jake.

Tamsen asked, "Did he give us any help? A map?"

"He did come part of the way back with me. He admitted that he had not explored the canyon trail before leading the Harlans and Youngs. It is not a good wagon trail. In narrow places there is scarcely room for a man on horseback to get through. His party had to build roads by chipping at the cliffs and building out over the edge of the raging water. They had to build windlasses on the top of the ridges to lift the wagons over. One wagon with its oxen slipped over the precipice and fell seventy-five feet. We saw the mass of ruins."

"So the Harlans and Youngs have already built those roads down the Weber. Why can't we just use them?" asked one man.

Reed just shook his head. "We could never lift our

wagons over the ridges."

"Not that Palace Car," said one man behind Tamsen.

Tamsen heard the sarcasm in his tone. She knew that many of the men resented James Reed and his aristocratic manner, his imperious ways, and his show of wealth symbolized by his elegant wagon.

"He puts on airs," was the common comment.

Yet Reed's logic prevailed. They decided to leave Weber Canyon before the gorge and follow the Indian trail that Hastings had pointed out to Reed.

Chapter 9

Early the morning of August 12 the Donner-Reeds left the Weber Canyon camp and followed the trail of the Harlan-Young wagons for only a half mile. They followed Reed's blazes. They went up rocky ridges, down into deep canyons, and up ridges again. They built roads. They hewed down twenty-foot alders, aspens, and willows. They built a windlass and pulled wagons over canyon walls. They double-teamed their wagons on the steepest slopes.

The men began to grumble. They were ox drivers, not road builders. There were only twenty-seven men and big boys to do the work.

Then on August 15 a new family of thirteen people caught up with them. That family added four workers for road building: fifty-year-old Franklin Graves, his driver, his eighteen-year-old son, and his son-in-law, Jay Fosdick.

Thirty-one workers now. Still one bad stretch of six miles took six days to build.

Days went by and still Stanton and McCutchen had not returned. Amanda was frantic and went to Tamsen with her worries.

"I'm afraid that Mac won't have enough food and I am afraid the Indians will kill him. Mary Graves was telling me about some friends of theirs, the Trimbles, who were traveling with them on the plains. She said that Mr. Trimble was killed by the Pawnees and that Mrs. Trimble and her children turned back to their old home."

Tamsen was worried, too, and turned to George. Strength seemed to come out of sharing with him.

George continued to share in the nursing of Luke, and he said after visiting him, "Luke admires you. He is quite interested in your box of school supplies. I think he would like something to read."

"I have a mystery story by Edgar Allen Poe. Maybe he would like that."

That evening as Tamsen lay on her blanket and George took his turn guarding the stock she thought how lucky she was. She and George were together. Poor Amanda. George was so kind and understanding to Luke, too. He was appreciative of compliments to her.

The next day the party pulled out of the canyon and reached the peak of a ridge. There was a shout of rejoicing. In the clear air just beyond another range of mountains they saw Salt Lake shimmering in the sun.

"There really is a Salt Lake," they exclaimed to each other.

Much of the tension subsided as they went down into the next canyon and there was no quarreling that day.

There was more cause for joy. Two emaciated men stumbled into camp. Amanda McCutchen rushed to her husband's arms sobbing happily.

Amanda's fears had been partly justified. The men had lost the trail and were starving. They were on the point of killing their horses for food when two friendly Indians found them, fed them, and accompanied them back to the trail.

"Were they Utes?" asked George. "Bridger said that the Utes were friendly. When we get to the desert we may meet with Diggers. They are not a tribe, he said, but renegade Indians."

Charles Stanton said, "I know you can see the Salt Lake from that ridge you just crossed, but the Indians said that we have to go down this canyon before we can cross the next ridge."

Now there was more road building by exhausted men. It took another week to cross the Wasatch mountains.

They were now three weeks behind the Harlan-Young party.

Once out of the mountains there was a drive across dry land. It was easy going for the wagons, but there was no vegetation for the stock. They came to a river flowing towards the lake. Following it they came to land that looked inviting to farmers like Jake and George. Would California be as good?

The camping place the night of August 29 was at the black rock by the shore of the Salt Lake where Reed, Stanton, and McCutchen had caught up with Lansford Hastings three weeks earlier.

The Donner wagons were the last to come in to the campgrounds. Tamsen and George were in the wagon with Luke Halloran, and Charles rode horseback behind them.

George leaned out of the wagon and whispered to Charles Stanton, "Pass the word along. Luke Halloran is dead. Tell James Reed that I have opened Halloran's trunk and found that he was a mason. Reed must conduct a masonic funeral."

The word passed. Death called the men to a unity that had been splintering for three weeks. They collected side boards from their wagons and in the morning the men made a coffin. Reed conducted the funeral. One of the men discovered a grave marked John Hargrave, August 6, 1846. They knew he must have been with the Harlan-Young party. They buried Luke beside him.

Tamsen and George looked over the contents of Luke's battered trunk. Luke had said that his horse, bridle, saddle, and trunk was to be George's. The masonic emblems had been on top. Under his clothes were a few keepsakes, and to their surprise, fifteen hundred dollars in gold and silver coins.

After the funeral Tamsen went to the wagon to air

out the blankets.

George scooped up the coins into a bag and said, "Let's hide the money somewhere in the family wagon. Little teacher, this money can be for your school. You've earned it."

He patted her on the shoulder and left, carrying the bag of money. He said he would take the masonic emblems to Reed.

Tamsen was pleased that George would give her the money. Then she thought about the feminists who lectured and wrote about women's property rights. George had said that she had earned the money. Yet it would not be hers until he gave it to her. Of course, that was legal. Money and property belonged to men to be stingy or generous with, as they wished.

When Tamsen told Elizabeth about the money, Elizabeth said, "That is your teapot money. You earned it."

"Teapot money? What's that?"

"When women earn money they save it in a teapot. Some call it their egg money if they earn it selling eggs. Our minister's wife calls hers the wedding money, for Reverend Jackson always gives her his wedding fee."

Tamsen thought that Elizabeth was talking like a feminist and didn't know it.

Chapter 10

After the funeral, in deference to the dead, the company delayed a day at the campsite. The next day they moved along the trail, avoiding the marshes, then around a range of mountains, and on the second day they reached a meadow and springs.

By one spring was a board with scraps of paper clinging to it. It must have been intended as a sign board, but most of the scraps were scattered around on the ground.

The emigrants were dismayed. Was this supposed to be a message left for them by Lansford Hastings, like the one in Weber Canyon?

"Maybe Indians tore it up," suggested one of the men.

Elizabeth's boys began picking up the fragments.

"Give them to your Aunt Tamsen," said Elizabeth. "Maybe she can read them."

The men stood around waiting while Tamsen pieced the scraps together.

"Yes, I'm sure it is Hastings's writing. It is the same as the note left at Weber Canyon. It says: Two days and two nights of hard driving to the next water and grass."

"The stock can't stand to be driven day and night!" said Jake.

"We will have to get all of our water barrels filled here at the spring and cut every smidgen of grass for the stock," said George.

"This must be the dry drive they spoke of at Fort Bridger. They said thirty-five or forty miles."

They spent the next day in preparation. The men cut grass and filled the barrels and drums with water for the stock. They filled buckets with drinking water.

Charles Stanton, who had no stock except his horse, filled his water bag with feed. He also helped the Donners. Meantime the stock grazed under the watchful eyes of Elizabeth's older boys.

The women cooked food. They were afraid there would be no fuel for more cooking for the next forty miles.

"More like fifty miles," said one man.

"Well, we've got enough grass for fifty miles, I'd say," said another.

Stanton said, "If we get an early start tomorrow morning, Thursday, we should get to water by Saturday sometime. The road looks pretty flat."

Early Thursday morning the wagons began to move along the Harlan-Young trail. The Reeds were at the end of the caravan. It was hard pulling for the oxen with the heavier load of supplies. So the Donners and the Reeds, who had ample provisions, got farther and farther behind the smaller wagons of the party. The oxen became exhausted.

There was a volcanic hill thrust up in the middle of the desert. The trail led them through the volcanic ash, and up a thousand feet, around the hill, with the oxen and the wagons still sinking in the ash. Finally they were out of the ash. The gravelly trail stretched on.

Thursday evening the emigrants drove late. The air was cooler. They had made from eighteen to twenty miles since morning. Spread out over a two-mile stretch, they stopped, watered their stock, rested through the cold hours of the night, and were on their way early Friday morning.

All day they struggled on. The lead wagon got through the dunes and traveled faster on the harder surface of salt. It was blazing midday by the time the Donners reached the salt flats. In the heat Tamsen climbed down and walked in the shadow of the wagon. George was walking by his team.

"Look," called George, "an oasis!"

Tamsen stepped up to his side, the heat slapping her face.

"Where?" she asked, her eyes searching the horizon.

"There. There! No, it's gone."

They turned to each other, saying simultaneously, "A mirage!"

Friday was a day of mirages. Stanton rode from the west on his horse.

He said, "Everyone is seeing mirages. William Eddy says he saw twenty men marching along. Some said they saw wagons with teams. At first they thought we were catching up with the Hastings party. A couple of the men wouldn't believe me when I told them they were seeing mirages. Well, I rode back to get a blanket. It was beastly cold last night."

"To think it would be so hot in the daytime and so cold at night," said George. "I heard that it was characteristic of the high deserts."

"Well, this is Friday. By tomorrow I hope we will have covered the forty miles," Stanton said, going to the Donner supply wagon to get his blanket.

He faced his horse west, patted his saddlebags, and said, "I hope we get to a water supply soon. There's not much left in these bags."

By Friday evening the Donners found both their drinking water and the water for the stock almost gone. Saturday morning there was no spring in sight.

Saturday noon and Eliza began to cry for water. Tamsen rationed out the last drinks to the girls, but soon they were moaning for more.

"Here, girls," she said as she dipped lumps of sugar in peppermint essence, "just suck it slowly. It will help."

"It's too bad the stock can't use that remedy," said George. "There's no water in the kegs."

Tamsen knew that George was beginning to worry. That increased her anxiety, for George was not easily perturbed. But he had a remedy for the girls.

"Here," he said as he handed each girl a flattened bullet, "chew on this. But mind, don't swallow it."

By Saturday night they seemed no closer to their goal, only farther behind most of the wagons. Only the Reeds were behind them.

Sunday noon James Reed, riding his horse Glaucus, caught up with them.

He said, "Our oxen have petered out. I told Matt and the drivers to give them what little food and water we have left, and drive them as far as they can take the weight of the wagons. Then they are to unhitch them and drive them to water. We must reach water today. I left Walter Herron to look after the family. I'm riding ahead with these water bags. I'll bring back water for them.

"Our girls are crying for water," said Tamsen.

"Give me your water bag. I'll bring back some for you."

After Reed left, Jake came over and he and George talked it over.

"Reed has the right idea. Let's unhitch the wagons and get the stock to water. Then we can come back for the family and the wagons," said Jake.

George, the teamsters, Jake, and his two stepsons left with all the stock except one horse. Tamsen, Elizabeth, and the children sought such relief from the scorching heat as the wagons afforded.

Soon Reed's teamsters, driving his stock, passed the

Donners' standing wagons.

"They look just about beat," said Elizabeth.

"We can't even offer them a drink of water," said Tamsen.

"Walter Herron isn't with them," said Elizabeth.

"No, Mr. Reed said he was leaving Herron to look after Margaret and the children."

"But she has her regular servants, Eliza and her brother, staying with her," said Elizabeth, shaking her head. "Society people! Even on the desert! Jake and George didn't leave a man for us."

"No. They seem to think we are capable enough."

"Of course. They know we don't need to have a man around just for the looks of things," said Elizabeth decisively.

Tamsen thought fleetingly that Elizabeth was more of a feminist than she realized, but she did not say anything. Her thoughts had to turn to her girls. She had to think of something that would help relieve their misery from the heat.

She brought out some of her stationery and colored pencils and they colored fans.

"Tamsen, don't let them use up all your writing paper. You need that for the things you write for the magazine," said Elizabeth.

"I have not had time for writing since we left Weber Canyon. Anyway no scouts have met us, and I have no way of getting my writings to the editor."

By noon there was so little shade by the wagons that the best they could do was crawl under them and endure.

"How can you write in your diary in all this heat?" asked Elizabeth.

"I haven't written but two words *Promethean heat.* That's a quotation from Shakespeare, from his *Othello.*"

"Whatever that means. It is a scorcher. How can you think of Shakespeare quotations at a miserable time like this?"

"Probably because I never was sure what the expression meant. *He used Promethean fire in Love's Labor Lost* which he said was from women's eyes This heat is so terrific it ought to have a strong name. But your word *scorcher* will do."

Just before daybreak Tamsen heard hoofbeats and Reed appeared, but not on Glaucus. He handed her the precious bag of drinking water.

Reed said, "I had to borrow this horse from Franklin Graves. Glaucus could scarcely make it."

"How far is it to water?"

"About twenty-five or thirty miles to a spring at the foot of Pilot's Peak."

"Have any of the others arrived at the springs?"

"Yes. Eddy's wagon arrived Saturday, but one of his oxen is lying out in the desert. Eddy has gone back to revive the critter, but I don't think it will survive. Franklin Graves arrived with his outfit on Saturday afternoon."

"The other emigrants?"

"I found them strung out along the trail, some with exhausted oxen still pulling their wagons. Others had unhitched their oxen, and leaving their families with their wagons, were driving their stock toward water. Other women and older children were plodding with the men and oxen. Their wagons looked like empty tombs. It was night by the time I finally arrived at the springs at the foot of Pilot's Peak. I put Glaucus to pasture, borrowed this horse from Franklin Graves, filled these water bags, and within an hour started back."

Chapter 11

All afternoon Tamsen and the girls sat in the shade of the wagon. Her thoughts were of George, suffering the full force of the sun. It seemed as if the desert had swallowed him. It was too hot to go over to Elizabeth's wagon and visit. The girls made paper fans.

"I'm thirsty," said Eliza.

"When will Mr. Reed bring us some water?" asked Georgia.

"Mr. Hastings said we would find water at forty miles." said Elitha. "Papa said we had already gone sixty or seventy miles."

"He said this morning it looks as if that peak is at least another ten miles," said Leanna.

"It's impossible to walk ten miles in this heat," said Tamsen, inwardly groaning.

"That'll be seventy or eighty miles when we get there," said Frances.

Tamsen thought Frances was ready for school. She was a good student. A fleeting thought of the school that she wanted to start in California came to mind.

By evening a cool breeze arose. For supper there was no milk, for the cows had been driven on with the stock. Instead of the usual supper of bread and milk it had to be hard biscuits and water. There were dried peaches and apples as usual.

By the time Tamsen had bedded down the little girls she realized they needed more covering. A cold wind was coming up. Since George was not there, Tamsen decided not to pitch the tent but to squeeze in beside the sleeping girls. Leanna and Elitha chose the space in the supply wagon where Luke Halloran had slept.

In the Reed wagon, some distance behind the

Donners, everyone was asleep except Margaret. She was nervous and restless.

James Reed awoke.

Margaret said, "I just can't sleep. It's cool now. Let's walk."

Her husband tried to dissuade her but Margaret's nervousness seemed to increase, and he was afraid that it would bring on her migraine. He said, "If I just had a horse for you to ride."

"I'd rather walk in the cool than blister in the heat."

"But Milt will soon be back with a span or two of oxen. He will take us in the wagon."

Reed finally consented and woke up the children. Virginia was eager to walk. They packed some food, mostly dried fruit and bread. There was some water in the bag that Reed had brought. Their hired help, Eliza and Baylis, carried blankets and extra shawls.

Four adults, four children, and five dogs started to walk, facing the cold wind. Cash, the children's pet, stayed close at Jimmie's heels. James Reed carried three-year-old Tommy while Margaret held Jimmie by the hand.

The wind increased. The children were soon exhausted and began to whimper. Reed feared Margaret was overtaxing herself.

Reed spread his blanket on the sand. As the little boys lay down Cash jumped between them. The dog and the boys cuddled together. Reed spread shawls over the four children, then ordered his other dogs to lie against the children. The adults wrapped up in blankets and sat with their backs to the wind, making a shield for the children.

Margaret rested her head on her husband's shoulder. They dozed uneasily.

Suddenly through the high notes of the wind there was a pounding sound. Reed sprang up alert. Four dogs leaped up. A dark creature came thundering toward them.

Reed felt a sudden terror. The sleeping children lay right in the path of the menacing creature. He dared not leave. He drew his pistol. The dogs made a mad rush at the approaching animal and it swerved.

As the animal dashed by Reed recognized that it was one of his own steers.

By this time the children were all awake and they ran in terror. By the time the children were rounded up and pacified the wind was beginning to die down. They all wanted to walk.

About six in the morning they arrived at the Donner wagons. The Donners were still asleep, so they crawled under the wagons and slept there until Tamsen Donner was awake.

Reed was anxious to get going and find out what was delaying his teamsters. Having been at Pilot's Peak he knew that the pasturage was good and the oxen should soon be ready to come back after the wagons.

Tamsen said, "Take Fanny. That's the only horse George left us."

"Doesn't she belong to the girls?"

Leanna spoke up. "Yes, she's ours. We aren't going out in all this heat, so you are welcome to her."

"Thank you. I'll stuff a little fruit in my pocket and get going while the morning is cool."

A few miles out he met George, Jake, and their teamsters. They had gone to Pilot's Peak, rested their stock, and were now coming back for their wagons. Jake had oxen for all his wagons, but George had too few.

Jake said to Reed, "Sorry to hear about your bad luck."

"What happened?" asked Reed greatly alarmed.

"Don't you know?" asked George. Your drivers are

out trying to find your stock. Billy Graves is helping them."

"Find my stock? Where? Why?"

"In the middle of the desert yesterday afternoon your horse Prancer collapsed. Your men were busy trying to revive him when all the stock, crazed by the heat and their thirst, went dashing in every direction."

"All of them? After midnight one of my steers came rampaging by and pretty nearly killed all of us."

Jake said, "Most of the other men have lost stock, too. Your men are out there now, trying to find some of them. So far all that they have found is one milk cow and one ox. Billy Graves is helping and he brought those in this morning."

"Are the other milk cows gone? Do I have a horse left?"

George said, "I think they revived Prancer. I saw Glaucus at the springs. She seemed to be in fair shape."

"That's something. I thought she'd be all right after a spell, so I left her at the springs."

George said, "Only these few yoke of oxen were fit enough this morning to do any pulling."

"I'll see that your family gets to the springs in one of my wagons," said Jake to Reed.

George and Jake with their teamsters and oxen continued on back to their families and wagons. Reed kept riding west to the springs. He learned that all of the emigrants except the Donners and his own family had arrived. Most of the men were out hunting missing stock. Thirty-six oxen, nineteen of them Reed's and some steers and horses had stampeded into the desert. Reed's teamsters had been out all night searching.

Meanwhile George and Jake had reached their wagons.

George said to Tamsen, "I brought back only two yoke of oxen. All the others were exhausted. So I will have to abandon one wagon. I told Sam Shoemaker to drive the family wagon with you and the girls. Jake and I will have to shift some supplies first, then I'll follow you with the other wagon."

Tamsen got her girls onto the wagon. She would alternately walk or ride. Jake found a place in one of his wagons for Margaret, her children, and her two servants, Eliza and Baylis.

As Tamsen walked, her thoughts were with George. He would have to load all their supplies in one wagon. That would overload it, so for the sake of his oxen, he would have to discard some things. Would he discard her box of school supplies? She thought, of course, it was his right--his legal right to do with them as he pleased. She wished success to all the feminists who were lecturing and agitating for women's rights.

While Jake helped George repack his baggage wagons, they sent the teamsters ahead with their family wagons. Margaret and her family rode with Jake's family.

Before starting, Elizabeth had seen that supplies for cooking their dinner had been put in the family wagon and a meal was ready by the time George, Jake, and their drivers arrived with two of Jake's wagons and one of George's.

Tamsen had tried to be philosophical about the loss of her box of school supplies, but still there was a sudden pang when she realized that George was not bringing in that wagon.

The Donners and Reeds ate together. George asked Reed what luck he was having finding his stock.

"Not much luck," said Reed. "Only one cow and one ox. I'm afraid the stock has died of thirst. If any of them reached water Milt thinks the Indians will already have captured them."

"I wish I could lend you a yoke of oxen to bring in your wagon," said George, "but it will be days before mine are ready."

"George had to leave one of our wagons in the desert," said Tamsen regretfully.

After supper as the heat of the day gave way to the cool of the evening, she walked to the edge of the desert and looked eastward. The reds and oranges of the sunset in the west paled to the soft grays in the east, desert and sky blending into each other. Except for the volcanic promontory, the desert stretched flat, sandy, and endless.

It was a desert of no return. In Tamsen's thought it stretched to the years she had left behind, to a comfortable home in Massachusetts, to her early love of books, to her teaching years in North Carolina, her brief marriage and motherhood. The pain of widowhood was now wrapped in the soft cloud of memory. She had George. Even the thought of the box buried in the sand did not dispel the glow she felt. George--he seemed to materialize out of her thoughts. But no, he was really there.

She felt his touch on her shoulder and then his arms around her.

"Little professor," said George, "we brought in your school supplies. Jake thought we ought to just leave it in the wagon bed and bury everything. But I talked him into taking my tool box into his wagon. Then we put your box in our other wagon."

Tamsen's spirits soared. She gave George a kiss. He had made her life whole. He had tied its fragments together and tied her future to his.

Chapter 12

At Pilot's Peak the stock that had survived the scorching desert had a week of rest with fairly adequate pasturage. The men had little rest. Some continued to search for their animals. Others returned to the desert for their wagons. All of the emigrants had lost some of their stock. Reed had lost nineteen working oxen, leaving him only one ox and one cow.

Reed's drivers continued to search for the lost animals. Reed borrowed two oxen to team with his surviving ox and cow. George returned to the desert with him.

Reed usually used four yoke of oxen for his big wagon and three yoke for each of his other two.

He said, "I can bring in only one wagon with these animals. I'll have to cache all my heavy stuff and take just food, clothes, and blankets."

They dug holes in the sand but salt water oozed out so they had to pile everything on the ground, fine furniture, boxes of books, tools, and household equipment. Then they heaped dirt and sand over the pile.

Reed said resignedly, "I doubt that we will ever get back here for this stuff."

"The Indians will probably find it," said George.

Back at the springs with the heavily loaded wagon, Reed realized that it was too much for his animals. The other drivers who had returned to the desert for their own wagons refused to take his heavy box of tools and equipment. Some of the families were short of food and offered to carry his supplies only if he would share with them. Even George could not carry anything now that he had only two wagons.

Tamsen said, "I think some of the men take

satisfaction that Reed has suffered the most loss. I heard one man say, 'That takes him down a peg.' Another said, 'He think he's somebody.'"

"They say he is descended from Polish aristocracy. Didn't you tell me that?" asked Elizabeth.

"Yes, he is. His family left Poland and went to Ireland. That's where he was born."

"Well, he is having it hard now, but when he gets to California he will probably make another fortune," said Elizabeth.

"All the men are pretty disheartened," said George. "They have lost so much. Their stock is all worn down to skin and bones. They do not cooperate."

Finally September 16 the emigrants were again on the trail. Their staples had been calculated to last to the end of September when they expected to reach California. They realized it would take more than two weeks, so they now began to worry about a shortage of food. They had heard about Captain Sutter in California. He had a reputation of being a friend of emigrants. They decided that someone should go ahead and buy supplies from him. George said he would guarantee payment. Charles Stanton and William McCutchen volunteered.

Stanton had his own horse. McCutchen had to borrow one. Soon they had ridden out of sight.

There was more desert to travel and then the trail became easier. There were treeless flat valleys, gaps in the hills, then springs. Occasionally one of the men bagged an antelope or mountain sheep.

This was Indian country. Bridger had called them Diggers, renegades who had no tribal connection. Most were shy. Others visited the camp, accepted gifts, and gave information about the location of springs. Some stole, usually a steer. One Indian stole Franklin Graves's shirt.

The Donners, whose wagons were in better shape, pulled ahead of the rest of the party and in a week were a day's journey in advance.

Every few days Reed rode ahead of the second section and talked with George and Tamsen. From his reports George learned some of the difficulties: the breakdown of wagons that had to be abandoned, and the death of stock.

"We are about ten miles back of you folks," Reed said. "Some Indians raided us the other night and got away with Eddy's ox. He had been lending me the critter. My ox and cow were not enough for my wagon so I had to borrow. Eddy's wagon went to pieces and they have been riding with us. Now I had to borrow again. I got one ox from Graves and another from Breen."

"How is Margaret," asked Tamsen.

"She is doing fairly well. I insist that she ride most of the time. To lighten the load for the animals Eleanor Eddy and Virginia walk with Eddy. Other women and their big children walk, too. They carry their cooking utensils and other items. The funniest sight," he added with a smile, "was Landrum Murphy. He was carrying a copper camp kettle on his head."

When Reed rode up to the Donners on September 28 the first thing he said was, "That Hastings is a fool. His trail brought us three days journey down the valley then three days back up north on this side of the range of hills."

George said, "I thought it was crazy, but I could not tell by my map."

"My map shows it as Ruby Range. We could have cut over the ridge in a day and so have saved five days."

"I felt in my bones that it wasn't right. That Hastings is crazy," said Jake angrily.

Chapter 13

Early next morning Tamsen was awakened by Georgia crying out, "Mamma! Mamma! The Indians!"

It was a nightmare again. Tamsen awakened her and comforted her. "It's all right, honey. You girls can just stay in the wagon while I go out and help your Aunt Elizabeth with the breakfast. Leanna can bring yours to you."

Soon pancakes and coffee were ready. The stock were grazing peacefully so the men came over for breakfast. George and Jake each came over with their buckets of milk which they handed to their wives.

"Not much here," said George, "I hope that they don't go dry."

Tamsen said, taking the bucket, "Here, Elitha, you take care of this milk, and here is some hominy. See that the little girls get most of the milk. Still you can use a little for your hominy. Then come back here, and I'll let you have some coffee."

Elizabeth said, looking in her bucket, "Is that all? Well, my little boys must have it. Elitha, stop at my wagon and tell Mary to come and get the milk. We will be going hungry soon. Look at the way my big boys eat! Almost as much as the hired men. Well, they earn it, helping with the stock. They eat more than George or Jake! Our flour is getting low. I hope the men get some game. We have not had any, even a goose, for three days."

"I saw an antelope," said Solomon, and coaxing his mother, added, "I bet I could get one if you let me have a gun."

Loud shouts came from the hill.

Indian heads popped up out of the sagebrush.

Arrows zinged through the air.

Animals bellowed as the arrows struck.

Some cows and oxen fell. Some animals with arrows sticking in them began racing around in a frenzy.

The men had stacked their firearms near the campfire when they had gone to breakfast. Now they grabbed them and repeatedly fired into the hills.

The children in the wagons screamed. Elizabeth and Tamsen rushed to the campfire to quiet their children's hysterics.

The animals began to stampede. Some of the men rushed after them while others went to the stricken animals. Twenty-one oxen had been struck by the arrows. Some were dead or dying. Some were too badly hurt to pull the wagons or even to keep walking on the trail.

There was just one thing to do. Jake Donner fired the first shot at his own oxen and George had to kill a milk cow and four oxen.

The men worked quickly, cutting meat from the carcasses of the beeves. Tamsen and Elizabeth roasted as much as they could use before it would spoil. The men had seen the Indians only when they stood up in the sagebrush. They ducked down and were gone.

It was noon before the party was on the trail. As they left, Elizabeth looked at the remains of the slaughtered animals and said, "Probably the Indians will come and feast on what we have to leave. Maybe their feasting will keep them so they won't follow us tonight."

The next day was September 30. This was the date when they had hoped to reach California. They knew most of the others were very low on food. Only Breen had carried an ample supply. Of course, James Reed had brought an adequate supply. However it was now stored in other wagons where it was being used up.

"We lost six days going down that valley," said Jake who was most ready to blame Hastings when things went wrong.

"We have two extra men to feed. Two of Mr. Reed's teamsters are with us," said Elizabeth.

"In this Indian country it is good to have extra night watchmen," said George.

At noon they came to a marshy stretch cut by a sluggish stream. On a stake was a board with two arrows. One arrow pointed north to F.H. and the other pointed east to S.L. The usual litter of a campsite was strewn around.

"This must be Humboldt," said George. Then F.H. means Fort Hall and S.L. means Salt Lake."

Elizabeth's boys went exploring. Nine-year-old Sonny, so called because his name was really George, said to his Uncle George, "I saw where someone had chipped a heart on a tree and it had the letters J.H. and E.A.F."

George laughed and said, "It looks as if some sparking was going on in one of the parties."

Sonny looked puzzled.

Tamsen explained, "Those initials are probably for Jake Harlan and Eliza Ann Fowler. They were in the Harlan party."

George said, "You are probably right. I'd guess that the Harlan-Young party was here about three weeks ago."

Solomon came over and said, "I saw a tree that had the date August 29th and the initials B.B. chipped on it."

Tamsen was stunned for a moment and exclaimed, "That was five weeks ago! That could have been someone in Governor Boggs's party."

"Well, let's get on the trail again. It looks now as if the pasturage will be good anywhere we want to stop. We'll be following the Humboldt for quite a spell."

Chapter 14

The trail left the Humboldt and turned west. The going was rougher: up steep hills, down to gullies, then up steep hills again.

Jake and George found that their teams were having difficulty going up a long steep hill. They were using two span of oxen for each wagon. Their extra oxen had been killed or stolen, so they decided to double-team with those they had. They double-teamed their spans, each in turn until all the wagons were across.

As soon as they found a place for good pasturage they camped.

The next day when the others came to this same steep hill they, too, decided to double-team.

The teamsters stood in line and waited for a turn. The two wagons of Graves's had gotten across and John Snyder was waiting in line for Graves to bring back a span from his second wagon to attach to his third.

Milt Elliott was in line after John Snyder. Since Graves had not yet returned with his oxen, Milt decided to start up the hill. Reed had borrowed a span that Milt had never driven, and as Milt tried to maneuver past John Snyder's animals they became unruly and tangled with them.

Snyder called Milt a fool. Sharp words followed. Snyder began to beat the oxen over the head. Reed rushed up, shouting at Snyder. Snyder's anger turned against Reed.

He cursed and said, "I'll cowhide you to hell."

Reed drew his hunting knife.

Alarmed, Snyder struck at Reed with the butt end of his whip, laying open a gash in his head.

Reed lashed out with his knife, striking Snyder just

below the collarbone.

Margaret rushed between them trying to separate them. Snyder continued fighting, striking Margaret once, and knocking Reed to his knees.

Snyder started away, then staggered. Young Billy Graves caught him. Reed staggered up, almost blinded by the blood from the gash. He went to the river and hurled his knife and staggered back to the prone Snyder.

"I didn't mean to kill you," he moaned. "Oh, I didn't mean to."

Snyder mumbled a few words and died.

Margaret and Virginia led Reed back to the wagon. Margaret was so upset that she let Virginia's steady hand attend to his wound. She bathed his forehead and bandaged his wound.

Meantime the men were standing around Snyder's body, expressing their shock. All petty irritations, the hardships, and resentments for weeks burst out.

Keseberg was coolly judgmental.

"Reed ought to be hanged," he said.

He deliberately disengaged the tongue from his wagon and propped it up with an ox-yoke. At first it seemed the men agreed with Keseberg. Then they hesitated about such drastic action. One suggested that they file murder charges when they reach California. If they killed him here they themselves could be charged with murder.

Keseberg was adamant. "No. We should hang him here."

He went ahead with his preparations.

When tempers cooled one man said, "We could banish him from the party."

Another said, "Let's banish him without food or a gun."

"His horse?"

"Glaucus? That broken-down racehorse. She'll soon conk out. Anyway she'd only use up food here."

Reed at first refused to leave but Milt and Eddy pointed out that his life would not be safe if he stayed. They promised to look after his family.

"Do go," said Margaret. "Your life is in danger here. You can bring food back to us."

Reed recognized the logic of that. He knew his life was not safe here. He would go.

Early the next morning before the others were up, Reed mounted Glaucus and left. About an hour later Virginia and Eddy, on horseback caught up with him. Eddy had brought him a gun and ammunition. Virginia handed him a small packet of biscuits.

She said, "Mamma didn't dare get any supplies from the other wagons. They might find out she was sending you something."

"I said I was going hunting so I'd better try to bring back something," said Eddy as he turned back.

With a last tight hug, Virginia left, and with a heavy heart Reed slowly rode on.

He reached the campsite where the Donners had camped the night but they were now on the road. He trudged on, berating himself for his actions.

Chapter 15

Elizabeth and Tamsen were preparing supper. George and Jake were tending the stock. Walter Herron and James Smith, Reed's hired men who were now traveling with the Donners, had gone off with their guns, hoping to get some wild geese, which were honking overhead.

Leanna and Eiltha were off looking for greens. Tamsen's three little girls were by the campfire, watching their mother and aunt and were hoping for tidbits. Mary had been sent to look after her three younger brothers. They were prone to wander and Mary had followed them.

Suddenly Mary came running and exclaimed breathlessly, "Look. There's a man coming on horseback."

George said, "His head is all bandaged."

Frances said, "It's Mr. Reed. I know because he is riding Glaucus."

Tamsen looked up with her mixing spoon poised in her hand.

James Frazier Reed. Could it be the aristocrat? The man looked more like a tramp. The horse looked as beaten as the rider. It was not the princely figure that was the Reed image.

George and Jake hurried to meet Reed. They stood by the wagon and talked.

Tamsen and Elizabeth silently watched. They saw George place his hand on Reed's shoulder. Jake shook his head, protesting something. Instinctively they knew the news was not good.

Walter Herron and James Smith came in with some geese. They handed them to Elizabeth and walked over to join the men. They, too, seemed to be disturbed by Reed's news.

Elizabeth began preparing the birds for roasting.

She said, "Tell George to invite Mr. Reed for supper. I'll fix a nice one."

Tamsen knew Elizabeth's usual way to show her sympathy was to offer good food. Her special treat for children was cookies.

The roasting of the geese delayed supper. Tamsen fed the children and put them to bed. Walter Herron continued in conversation with Reed. George came to Tamsen and told her what Reed had told him about Snyder's death.

Tamsen was shocked. She was not a judgmental person. Her sympathy was first with the victims, Snyder and Reed both.

She said, "Snyder was such a high-spirited young man. He was somewhat of a charmer with the young women."

"Yes, but he had a quick temper."

"Poor Margaret! It's terrible. How will she get along without her husband?"

It was dark by the time supper was ready.

The October evening chill was in the air, and after supper they lingered around the fire.

Tamsen watched Reed's face in the flickering firelight. Pain had deeply etched it. Her heart ached for him.

There was silence for a time. Reed had already told his story and seemed unwilling to elaborate.

"It will be hard on Margaret without you," said Tamsen sympathetically.

He murmured, "Oh, Margaret, oh my dear."

The words faded away. His inward communication was with Margaret. The words were not for Tamsen, but she had seen the look in his eyes. Her sense of poetry wanted to name that look but all words seemed to have wings. She had glimpsed a man's love for his wife and a something between them which another was rarely permitted to see.

Walter Herron said to George, "We have talked it over. I am going with him. I can walk. Glaucus is about ready to drop. Soon we will be walking together."

"I'm glad you are going with him," said George. "I'll patrol tonight." To Reed he added, "Smith and Herron have been a great help patrolling at night. We have to be on the lookout for Indians. I hate to ask the teamsters to drive all day and then patrol at night."

Tamsen said, "You two can sleep in our tent tonight. George will be on patrol, and I'll crawl in beside my little girls."

Leanna and Elitha had been sleeping in the other wagon where the extra blankets were stored. Tamsen decided to give Reed a blanket, for he had been sent away without one. She went to the wagon and found the girls awake and giggling.

"What is tickling your funny bones?" she asked.

Leanna said, "We want you to ask Mr. Reed something."

Reed was standing just outside. Leanna pulled the curtain aside.

Elitha, controlling her giggles, asked solemnly, "Why do you call your horse Glaucus? She's a mare and you should call her Glauca."

Their heads popped back and Leanna closed the curtain.

"I see your girls know their Latin," said Reed with a smile. "I hope you get your school started."

"Yes," said George, putting his arm across

Tamsen's shoulder. "My little professor. You should see all the school supplies stowed away in this wagon."

This little levity helped ease the day's tension. The two men were soon asleep.

Tamsen slept only fitfully. She was thinking of Margaret and how she must be suffering. Again the look on Reed's face came to mind. There was something special in their relationship. That poetic expression which had eluded her came now to mind--precious pearls, pearls of great price. But that was a biblical reference. Her mind struggled for another quotation. Keats? Browning? No. She came back to pearl--a pearl of great price. But what price? A quotation from Henry Ward Beecher's sermon came to her: It is the suffering element that measures love. Margaret and James Reed were suffering. Was that the price of his love for Margaret that she had seen in his eyes?

Tamsen realized that there had been a growing love between herself and George. Was there a deeper love--a pearl of great price?

She had already paid a price. Maybe someday society would let a woman be a wife and have a career. A few women were striving to combine the two. But to combine motherhood and a career? Hopefully she could in California. On the whole she had not had to pay the price that many women paid in marriage. George was already well-to-do. She had luxuries that many women did not have until later years. George had been cooperative in her school plans. If she had not married him she could have gone to Oberlin College. It allowed women students now.

Georgia thrashed around in her sleep, and Tamsen found her position uncomfortable. She climbed out of the wagon, carrying a large shawl.

Coffee was being kept warm over a low fire.

Tamsen went over and poured a cup. George joined her. Then he put the shawl over both their shoulders and they walked away from the wagons.

Except for George's one comment, "Poor Reed," they walked in silence, each buried in his own thought.

Tamsen knew that George had no words for his deepest emotions. She had learned that his light teasing and his pet names for her were his way of expressing love. Those were the pearls she had over the years.

George drew her close, leaned over, buried his face in her hair, and murmured, "At least we are together."

"Yes, together," Tamsen whispered. It was a commitment each to the other.

This is my pearl of great price, thought Tamsen.

Chapter 16

James Reed and Walter Herron left early the next morning ahead of the Donners.

In the next few days some of those behind the Donners pressed forward, drove through the night, and caught up with them. Margaret Reed and her family and William Eddy's family rode together in a wagon borrowed from Franklin Graves. The oxen were Eddy's.

Margaret came to the Donner wagon. It was the first time Tamsen had seen her since Reed had gone on ahead.

Margaret said, "I worry about Mr. Reed. We are afraid the Indians might kill him. I'm afraid he won't get enough to eat. The girls and Milt scouted around and they have found signs that he has killed a goose. He left a note that the Indians were skulking in the bushes. I guess they are looking for something to steal and he doesn't have anything worth stealing."

"Did you know that Walter Herron is with him?" asked Tamsen.

"Oh. I'm glad. Mr. Reed thinks a lot of Walt, and Milt, too. They are like family. As for the servants, well, they do what they can, but they, especially Eliza, are more like children to be taken care of."

On the morning of October 13, while scarcely daylight, the Indians pounced again striking down eighteen cattle and one milk cow. While most of the animals belonged to the Donners, others suffered losses. There was near panic.

The men hastened to cut off steaks and after a hasty breakfast most of the families were on the trail again. But there were those who had lost all their oxen and had to stop to bury their wagons and supplies in the sand.

Elitha and Leanna were out helping Tamsen and Elizabeth get breakfast. They saw Virginia Reed and went over to talk to her.

When they returned Elitha said to Tamsen, "Mr. Eddy lost his oxen and he hasn't any to draw his wagon. Mrs. Reed and Virginia are putting some of the bags of clothes and things in the Breen's wagon."

"Will she be riding with them?"

"No. Virginia said they would have to walk."

"You tell them to come and walk with us. Papa and your Uncle Jake are cutting some steaks, and as soon as we can, we must be on the road."

Margaret came over to the Donner wagon and waited for Tamsen.

She said, "I've put the little boys on the horses. Virginia, Patti, and Milt will walk beside them. Poor Eddy. His oxen are all gone, stolen, or killed by the Indians. It's Graves's wagon but he can't spare oxen to pull it. Eddy is burying his supplies, even his broken gun, but he is taking bullets and his powder horn. He hopes to borrow a gun. All the food the Eddys can carry is three pounds of sugar."

Elizabeth said, "The Breens, Graves, and the Murphys have started already. Who is that women walking with them?"

"I think it is Mrs. Wolfinger," said Tamsen.

George came over to the women and said, "The wagon will be moving out in a few minutes. We simply can't delay any longer. I understand Wolfinger's oxen were killed and he is burying his stuff."

"Mrs. Wolfinger has already left walking with the women," said Tamsen.

Jake said, "Some of the Dutchmen have lost oxen and are burying their wagons. They can look after each other and double up. I understand Keseberg still has his wagon and oxen."

It was midmorning by the time the Donners left. It looked as if Eddy with his wife and children and his three pounds of lump sugar might soon be following.

If one could have added up all the miseries of the eighty tattered and disheveled people on the trail from the Humboldt sink to the Truckee River, the total would have been staggering. Individually, for most it was the little things that compounded their miseries: the step-by-step agony as they sank in ash almost to their knees; the step-by-step torture as the trail crossed ridges of volcanic rock which cut through their moccasins; thirst that could be slacked only by the brackish water carried from the sinkholes of the Humboldt; the searing heat beating down where there was no shade; and the glaring sunlight that the desert threw back in their faces.

For two of the men it was more than the little things. For old man Hardkoop it was death when his lacerated feet could carry him no farther and no one would give him a lift. For Wolfinger it was death when he had to bury his wagons and no one would go back for him.

By evening they had not reached a resting place. The moon rose so they struggled on until they reached Geyser Springs. There they halted until morning.

Geyser Springs was a diabolic place. At intervals steam jetted twenty feet into the air. The men caught the water in buckets. They let it cool and watered their stock. The water tasted bitter.

George brought Tamsen a pitcher of the hot water and she brewed some coffee. It was barely palatable.

Tamsen, Elizabeth, Margaret, and the men hastily had their breakfast of coffee and dried-out biscuits.

The men brought in the oxen and hitched them to

the wagons.

The children were awake, and the women took biscuits and even coffee to them.

"I don't approve of coffee for children ordinarily," said Tamsen.

"It is the only way they will drink the water," said Elizabeth.

The Eddys, William and Eleanor, arrived walking. They were exhausted from carrying their children.

"Does anybody have water?" called Eddy.

"Just some hot water cooling over there in that pitcher," said Elizabeth. "But wait, I'll give you some coffee and you can brew it. It doesn't taste too bad."

"The water tastes bitter," said Tamsen, "so I'm letting even the children have some coffee."

"Thanks," said Eddy. "They have had nothing but sugar to suck on. Do you have any idea how far it is to the Truckee River?"

"George says it is about twenty more miles."

There was a loud sound of men discussing and swearing. Tamsen, alarmed, joined the men.

George said, "These critters can hardly drag themselves, let alone so much weight. We will kill them if we don't lighten it."

"This is the heaviest," said Sam Shoemaker, his hand on a box.

"The school supplies," said Tamsen in an agonized voice.

George put his arm around her shoulders, and whispered, "Little professor, I am sorry. We still have the quilt with the ten thousand dollars. That will be your building fund." Turning to the men he said, "We must bury this deep."

He shook his head as his voice trailed the words, "If

we can ever get back for it. . . ."

Again the Donners and Reeds were on the move. The oxen were struggling along. The adults walked, dragging their feet through the ash. They choked from the ash rising in the air. They passed three dead oxen from the forward wagons. They passed three men of their party whom Jake called the Dutchmen. They were burying a wagon.

As Tamsen trudged beside their wagon she carried the burden of a dead dream in her heart.

Chapter 17

October 15 and there was cool, sweet water at last. The Truckee River rushed down from the Sierras. Bottomland grass and wild peas made luxurious pasturage for the stock. Cottonwoods grew tall. The Truckee was the river of Heaven itself.

The emigrants judged by the campfires that the Harlan-Young party had taken sixteen days to cover the distance they had made in twelve days. So in spite of their remembrances of their hardships, they now began to congratulate themselves. Yet there was an urgency to move on. The nights were chilly, and they were afraid of the coming of snow. The cattle were dispersed over the meadow but that made them easy prey to the Indians. Those with the most cattle left were the most inclined to linger.

Most of the families were low on food. The Eddys had no food at all. There had been no game in the desert. When Eddy heard the honk of geese, he borrowed a gun and in two hours he brought down nine geese which he shared with the other families. He and his family ate with the Donners.

Elizabeth said to Tamsen, "I hope some of these people have a twinge of conscience when Eddy shares."

"Yes, I agree with you," said Tamsen. "These same people refused to give food to Eddy's children when they were hungry, yet Eddy shares his food with them."

After the meal Tamsen and Elizabeth checked the supplies for breakfast.

Tamsen said, "Surely Stanton and McCutchen will be coming soon. We don't have much food left."

Elizabeth said, "They have been gone a month. You'd think they would be back by this time if they could buy supplies from Mr. Sutter."

Eleanor Eddy said, "Some people in the other wagons wonder if they will come back at all. I think Mr. McCutchen would. His wife is so nice and Harriet is so cute. She's a year old, just the age of my Margaret."

"Yes," said Elizabeth. "Surely he would come back for them. He knows they didn't have much food on hand. But Stanton--he doesn't have any family."

"He's a gentleman," said Tamsen defensively. "I'm sure he can be depended on."

George looked at Tamsen quizzically, and then said, "Of course, he is a gentleman. Why so defensive?"

Elizabeth looked sharply at Tamsen and said, "Don't let the gossips bother you."

Tamsen asked, "So what do the gossips say?"

Elizabeth shrugged as she answered. "They say he wrote notes to you."

"He writes poetry and he likes to have me read it," said Tamsen.

"He writes more than poetry," said George. "He is interested in geology and he makes notes about that."

Tamsen smiled. George paid no attention to gossip. He had no place in his heart for petty jealousy. He was thinking of more important things.

He said, "I hope he can make a deal with Sutter. I promised to pay for anything they can buy. Stanton and McCutchen have been facing the same perils as we have. The Indians would be glad to get their horse and mule."

The next day they were on the trail up the Truckee River. Never again would they be without water. The river spilled down to the bottomlands through a twisty range of rocky hills. They had to go up narrow canyons and ford the river back and forth.

The third day Charles Stanton with seven pack

mules carrying supplies and accompanied by two Indians came down the trail.

Tamsen had a feeling of triumph. She had said that Stanton would not fail them. He had lived up to the standards of a gentleman. What about McCutchen? Stanton said he was ill and was staying at Sutter's Fort. He would come as soon as he was able.

There was rejoicing among the families who had gotten this far on the trail. Fires were built under the Dutch ovens and there was the smell of fresh bread.

Margaret Reed's family, the Donner families, the teamsters, and Mrs. Wolfinger gathered around the Donner campfire to listen to the news.

Stanton said, "That Sutter is a prince of a fellow. He gave us all this flour and beef jerky and his workers are taking care of McCutchen. These Indians--he calls them *vaqueros*--work for him. They are Catholic. They don't speak English, just Spanish. I promised to return them and the mules."

Margaret asked anxiously about her husband.

"Yes, I'm sure James Reed and Walter Herron got through to Sutter's Fort. They almost starved to death. Then they caught up with the Harlans and Youngs who gave them some food. I met the Harlan-Youngs when they were about two days travel from Sutter's Fort. Reed and Herron had just arrived at the camp. I talked with Reed while I was there. He said his horse gave out, and they had to leave her to die."

"Oh, poor Glaucus," said Virginia.

"Papa is all right," said Patti throwing herself in Margaret's arms.

There were tears in Margaret's eyes, and Tamsen rejoiced with her.

The next morning Charles Stanton went farther

down the Truckee trail to bring a share of the supplies to the families in the rear.

Returning to George Donner's wagon, Charles told George, "I'm going to use these mules to take Margaret Reed's family. She hasn't any wagons left and has only two horses that are scarcely fit for travel. She has four children and two servants that she is responsible for. With my seven mules we can make it by having the children ride behind the adults."

"How are the roads?" asked George.

"There has been some snow already in the Sierras, but so far it has melted."

When Mrs. Wolfinger left the circle around the campfire Stanton lowered his voice and asked, "Have you heard what they are saying at the other campfire about Wolfinger? Do you think he was murdered?"

George hesitated. Tamsen knew he suspected the stories were true, but she knew he was always hesitant to accuse anyone.

George answered, "You see, Wolfinger's oxen were killed by Indians so he had to bury his wagon. Some men stayed to help him. When they caught up with us they said he would be along soon. Nobody had a horse to spare to go back for him. We waited overnight but he never came. His wife was walking with the women, carrying a heavy load. We invited her to put her bag in our wagon and walk with us. I know the gossips are now saying that the men who stayed back with him must have murdered him for his money."

Elizabeth also added, "Gossips say that he was very rich. Mrs. Wolfinger has such beautiful clothes and she used to wear loads of jewelry. If she has any money left it is hidden away in the padding of her clothes. She never has anything to say."

"Her bustle is awfully big," said a voice behind Tamsen.

She turned quickly and realized that Elitha, Leanna, and Virginia were listening.

They looked embarrassed and quickly moved away. They took the younger girls by the hand and went over to watch the *vaqueros* with their mules. Charles Stanton left with Margaret to collect her belongings that she had left in the Breen's wagon.

"It looks as if Leanna, Elitha, and Virginia are paying a lot of attention to Mr. Stanton," said Elizabeth.

"Yes," said Tamsen, "the girls are growing up. Mr. Stanton is thirty-five but he looks younger. He is very attractive. I'd rather the girls begin to notice a nice refined man like Mr. Stanton than the young teamsters in the party. I imagine Mr. Stanton has always been attractive to women."

By this time Margaret had gathered together her few belongings and taken them to the men for packing on the mules. Their bedding, some food, and a few household articles were all her possessions. Margaret rode a mule with her three-year-old Tommy. Five-year-old Jimmy and eight-year-old Patti rode behind the *vaqueros*. Virginia rode behind Charles Stanton. They departed ahead of the Donners.

Chapter 18

The Donners followed the twisty trail up the Truckee River and on October 20 arrived at Truckee Meadows. Tamsen was surprised that they had caught up with Charles Stanton and the Reeds, who had made better time with the mules. She, Elizabeth, George, and Jake went over to have a chat with them.

"How's the trail from here on?" asked George.

"There's rich grasslands like this for a day's journey. Then we'll have to cross the river."

"Again!" exclaimed Jake. "We have been crossing back and forth time and again."

"Forty-eight times in eighty miles," said George.

"After we cross the river the next time the trail goes sharply to the right, away from the river across a fairly easy range of mountains into a beautiful little valley. Then the trail crosses another easy divide and gets into rolling country until it gets to Lake Truckee. You can see the pass above the lake. The pass is a humdinger. There's a cabin beside the lake."

"A cabin?" Elizabeth said questioningly.

"They say it was built by a man named Schallenberg two years ago because the pass was clogged with snow."

"What is the pass like?" asked George.

"It is broken domes of granite. It's steep. It's worse than the Wasatch to get wagons across."

Jake said, "We had to use a windlass and ropes to get over the canyon walls in the Wasatch and we had to double or triple the oxen teams."

"The Youngs and Harlans had to do the same to get over this pass." He slapped the rump of a mule and said proudly, "These critters made it all right."

The weather had been cloudy all morning and was

now threatening.

I think we should be moving on," said Elizabeth to her husband.

"But we should build up our stock for the hard climb," said Jake.

George agreed. He said, "Our oxen need to be in better shape to get over that pass. We will have to double up to do it."

"But the weather," said Tamsen. Tamsen was really worried, but certain decisions belonged to the men. Their stock came first, for they were farmers.

By this time the other families, the Breens, Graves, and Murphys, reached the meadows.

The weather continued to threaten and everyone was nervous. For five days they argued. Meantime the stock grazed.

Tamsen wondered why Stanton was delaying. He seemed loath to leave his friends. He talked with George about the geology of the country. He described the Sierra trail west of the pass. He seemed delighted with the tall pines which surrounded the valley.

"I'm going for a stroll over the meadow. Want to go along?" he asked Tamsen.

"Yes, I would enjoy it. We might find something to cook for greens. I'm sure the girls would enjoy it, too."

The girls were not far away whenever she was near Stanton and now they responded quickly to her invitation. Tamsen was glad to have them along. She was always pleased when the girls showed interest in botany. Today it occurred to her that, if the women in the other wagons were watching, it would still any gossip which might arise if she and Stanton were seen exploring the meadow alone.

Tamsen watched the girls. She realized that they adored Stanton, yet they were too young to practice any wiles. They clung together for support. Stanton treated the young girls with just the right degree of courtesy and attention. It was the mark of a gentleman.

Still Tamsen wondered why he did not go ahead even though his friends, particularly George, delayed. He could have been ten miles closer to the pass by this time. What excuse did he have for delaying?

George said, "His mules are in good shape, and they can scramble over rocks in the pass."

When Stanton joined the Donners he looked distressed and said, "Can't these people see that they have to work together or perish separately?"

"Yes, it looks like every family for itself. You could go on ahead with the Reeds."

Stanton replied, "People are going to need help at the pass. My mules can make it. If any of the others can't make it in time, I could get the Reeds to Bear Valley and then go back and help the rest get across. They are going to have to double-team to get over."

"A devil's chance of that," exclaimed Jake. "It was fighting over taking turns that caused the trouble. Oh I beg your pardon."

He turned apologetically to Mrs. Reed.

Tamsen saw the hurt that came into Margaret Reed's eyes. Jake's remark had reminded them all of that tragedy.

"How about snow in the pass?" asked George.

"There was a little snow in the mountains on October seven. The Harlan-Youngs were caught in it, but it melted right away. The heavy snows don't come until the middle of November."

"There was snow over two weeks ago," said Elizabeth with a shiver.

"The stock need a couple more days to feed," said

Jake decisively.

"Mrs. Breen said her husband is anxious to get moving. They are going to start tomorrow."

The next morning the wagons of the Breens and Graves began to move. George noticed that Stanton began to get his party ready as soon as the Graves hitched up their oxen. Tamsen regretfully said good-bye to Margaret's family. Her two stepdaughters solemnly watched Virginia's departure. She was again riding the mule behind Charles Stanton.

George slapped his legs and exclaimed, "By golly, that explains it! I now see why Stanton didn't skedaddle out of here with his Indians and his mules."

Jake winked and grinned. Tamsen looked puzzled.

"Yes," said Jake. "He's been sparking her."

"Who is sparking what girl?" questioned Tamsen sharply. She was certain they were talking about Charles Stanton. She thought, no, no, not the girls. Not sparking them.

"Stanton and Mary Graves sparking. Would you believe it?" said George.

"That's a pretty one. She is twenty years old. I was talking to her married sister, Sarah Fosdick," said Elizabeth. "I guessed there was a little romance there."

Leanna and Elitha listened to this conversation silently. Catching the look that passed between them, Tamsen was sure they knew more than they would say.

The chill of the air and the threat of snow worried Tamsen. She wanted the men to abandon everything and get over the pass, but she realized that they were not ready to do that. Still if their wagons got caught in the pass, Stanton and his mules would be able to get them across.

It was a day later, October 29, when the Donners were ready to move. With them were Mrs. Wolfinger,

Jean Baptiste Trudeau, James Smith, Noah James, Sam Carpenter, and Joseph Reinhardt. The latter, whom Jake still called the Dutchman had lost his oxen and wagon.

On a steep downward grade, an axle broke on George's wagon. Household goods slipped into a heaped-up mass. Bedding was in a tangle. Georgia was trapped and began screaming. George quickly untangled the bedding and pulled her out, but there was no sign of Eliza.

"Eliza, my baby. Eliza," called Tamsen frantically.

Jake came over to the wagon and all the men dug madly into the heap of goods. At last they found Eliza, limp, smothered, and unconscious.

Tamsen bathed her face with cool water and held smelling salts to her nose. She soon revived.

When the men were assured that no bones were broken they went to the serious task of repairing the axle. Tamsen sat on the heap of spilled blankets and cuddled Eliza.

For a while Tamsen was unaware of the growing threat of snow. Her whole concern was centered in Eliza.

It was noon, and Elitha and Leanna brought out some milk and buns for themselves and for Frances and Georgia. Eliza dashed from her mother's arms to her sisters, demanding some buns, too.

Tamsen breathed a sigh of relief.

Chapter 19

George and Jake cut timber for a new axle. They started shaping it with a chisel.

Jake said with a shiver, "It's getting colder every minute. I wouldn't be surprised if we get a humdinger of a snowstorm by tonight. We got to get moving."

George said, "A couple of the drivers thought we ought to abandon everything, put the children on the horses, and make for the pass. Let the cattle fend for themselves."

"Danged city fellows. A farmer doesn't leave his stock," said Jake indignantly.

Jake and George simultaneously screamed. The women rushed to them. Jake, cursing, threw down the chisel and kicked it. Blood was spurting from George's hand.

"Blood!" said the women. "What happened?"

"Just a little cut," said George.

"The chisel slipped," said Jake, kicking the tool again.

Tamsen hurried for her box of medical supplies. She used a salve and bound up George's hand with muslin strips. She was worried because it was such a long, deep cut. It was just like him to minimize its seriousness. He pooh-poohed her concern.

He said, "There are other things to be more concerned about than a measly cut. We must finish making this axle and get the wagons going."

After putting the new axle in place, they moved on. It began to snow and soon the trail was obscured.

George said, "I'd guess we are about five or six miles from the cabin Stanton told us about. This must be the trail that leads to Truckee Lake just below the pass, but in this snow I can't see the pass."

"I think we should veer to the right," said Noah James.

"No, to the left a little," said James Smith. "Before it snowed I could see what must be the pass."

"We just have to camp here," said George, "and build some kind of shelter. We can't move until this storm is over."

Jake said, "You're right. Anyway there are plenty of trees nearby to fix up some kind of shelter in a jiffy."

George drove his oxen close to a big pine tree.

Tamsen said, "Elizabeth and I will have to keep the children in the wagons until you get something built."

"None of you menfolk can sleep on the ground tonight," said Elizabeth. "You'll have to roll up in the supply wagons."

The men hurried out with their axes and soon had a supply of logs. It continued to snow and they spent the night in the wagons.

The next morning it was still snowing. In spots snow was three feet deep, so the task of cutting the trees and dragging them in would be too time consuming. They hastily built shelters with the materials on hand. George scooped a hollow at the base of the large pine tree for a fireplace. He placed his tent south of the tree and then erected a lean-to with the tree as the north wall. He framed it with logs and branches and covered it with quilts, rubber coats, hides, and buffalo robes. Jake built a similar shelter at the base of a pine tree at a little distance. Across a small creek the other four men built a sort of Indian wigwam where they could sleep.

The hovels were cold and damp.

Tamsen and Mrs. Wolfinger built a fire to take off the chill and to warm up some food. The girls stayed huddled in the bedrolls in the family wagon. Before George could come in out of the cold he and Sam Shoemaker had to cut wood for the fireplace.

Tamsen and Mrs. Wolfinger scooped out the snow on the floor of the lean-to and tent but the residue left the floor cold and muddy.

When George came in, Tamsen said, "I can't let the girls out of the wagon. The floor just churns up into cold mud."

"I'll fix that," said George.

He drove stakes into the ground and made a frame of poles over which he laid the side boards taken from his wagon. He now had a platform a foot above the ground. On this he put blankets and bedrolls.

It continued snowing the next day.

George took out some sacks of fodder for his stock. He could see only one ox and one horse through the curtain of snow. He could hear that Jake was out, too, and he called to him.

When Jake came to him, George said, "I'm afraid some of our stock have wandered off. In this deep snow they can't walk very far. I am worried about feed. I haven't much fodder left."

"Neither have I," said Jake. "I never saw a storm like this. It should clear soon."

Returning to the shelter, George said to Tamsen, "You can't see your hand before your face. The critters have wandered off, but there are clumps of trees out there. I hope they have found some shelter. Just so it doesn't freeze."

The next day it rained. That pleased George. The snow had now totaled about six feet, but the rain should melt it down to manageable levels so men and beasts could move over it.

That night it froze.

In the morning George went out in the falling snow. Tamsen heard his voice but could not at first understand what he said. Then she realized that he was cursing angrily. As a woman, of course, she should pretend not to hear. She knew that such language was used around the barns, but George was too much of a gentleman to use it in front of a woman.

"The animals have frozen to death," said George as he entered.

Since Tamsen was afraid that would happen, the words were not so much a shock but a knell, slowly ringing, benumbing her.

George added, "On account of the snow I can't see many of them. I dug out two horses and an ox. The snow is so deep that the others are just buried in it."

Alternate freezing and snowing continued for eight more days, until November 11. The shelters were completely covered with snow. They were prisons open to the air only at the trees where the warm air rose from the fires.

The men among the three groups were occasionally able to slog through the snow to each other's camps and to explore for wood. The snow piled up on the roof of the shelter. They were afraid the weight would crush it.

Snow covered the carcasses of the animals that had frozen to death, and George and Jake were able to find only two of them. Although the animals had been starving, their bodies furnished some meat to feed the twenty-one hungry people in the shelters.

George literally worked out his anger and frustration by the almost ceaseless activity of butchering the beeves and chopping wood. He would not admit that the cut on his hand was serious enough to slow his activities. He insisted that sponging was all the care his hand needed.

Tamsen protested. Finally he accepted her medication. She went to her chest of medical supplies and got a bottle of turpentine and sponged his hand. He winced, but let her repeat sponging.

Chapter 20

Jake had told Tamsen that she was too much a worrier. She had worried when their party had left the larger emigrant party at Little Sandy. But as time went by she dispelled her anxieties by the activities of each day.

Tamsen's feeling of panic, which had been triggered when the axle of the wagon broke and the little girls were pitched out in a smothering bundle of bedding, and had been augmented by the accident to George's hand, had now subsided to a nagging worry. She felt trapped in this hole of a shelter.

She realized George, too, had moments of fear when he found his stock frozen. But after his first burst of cursing and a few days of feverish activity he was again his normal self.

Tamsen did not garner hope from his attitude as much as she acquired acceptance of a philosophy that one did one's best. Philosophy or religion? She doubted George thought of it as either. He had been a member of the German Reformed Church, and he reflected their attitude without analysis. Now as she and George had to face an unknown future she found strength in his strength.

On November 11, when the storm seemed to be clearing, George began talking of plans.

He said, "I figure that some of the party, at least the Reeds and Stanton, have got over the pass."

He brought out the map that Stanton had drawn for him and pointed. "Here is the cabin Schallenberg had stayed in winter before last. Now if we could move up that far."

"But we have no oxen," said Tamsen, looking anxiously at George.

"Yes," he said. "But I've figured they could not

have got all their animals over the pass. Stanton seemed to be afraid that they couldn't get the stock across and that his mules would be the only animals able to make it in the snow. I'm only guessing. I think I'll make a trip to the lake. Now that the storm is over, six miles wouldn't be too much of a trek. If Breen or Graves are still there I might be able to buy some oxen from them."

"What if they are gone and the animals are frozen?"

"They would have more shelter there for their animals than we had."

"Please, George, send one of the men. Your arm worries me. Send Sam Shoemaker or James Smith."

Sam went to the lake that afternoon. When he returned the next day the sun was shining. Everybody came out of the shelters to hear his report. In a moment all the small children were scampering in the snow. But Elitha and Leanna stood by Tamsen.

Sam said, "They are all camped by the lake. Nobody got across the pass."

"Not even Stanton with his mules?" asked Tamsen. "Oh, if he had only gone ahead with Margaret and her family, and not waited for the rest."

Sam said," Well, the Breens and the Eddys were ahead of everybody. They got to the lake first. They kept on going. They went along the north shore of the lake. The road was so close to the edge that they were afraid the wagons would topple off into the water. They guessed they were three miles from the summit. The snow was five feet deep and they couldn't tell where the trail was. They turned and went back to the cabin by the lake.

"The next day there was pouring rain. By evening the rest of the wagons got as far as the lake. Stanton was with them."

"I guess Stanton stayed pretty close to the Graves's

wagon," said Jake.

"Well, yes," said Sam. "The next morning the weather was better, so Stanton and about half of the others started up the trail. The oxen petered out. They left their wagons and packed some of their things on the oxen and mules. They got almost to the pass, but the animals sank in the snow knee-deep. Stanton and one Indian went ahead to find the trail. They got over the divide but Stanton came back for the rest."

"Of course, he would come back for his friends," said Tamsen.

Sam said, "By the time he got back it was dark and it was snowing. The whole caboodle of them were tuckered out. They settled down for the night in their blankets right in the snow. By morning the snow had covered the trail again so they went back to the cabin by the lake. The Breens had not been with them, but had already moved into the Schallenberg cabin. The Kesebergs built a lean-to. The others made themselves shelters of poles, hides, and canvas--hardly better than we have here."

"How are they for food?" asked Tamsen.

"Their supplies are almost gone."

"Can they fish in the lake?" asked Jake.

"They can see some fish, but they are not biting."

"Stanton told me that it would be mountain trout. The fellows don't have the equipment, nor the know-how to fish for trout," said George. "Have they found any game?"

"Eddy killed a coyote, an owl, two ducks, a gray squirrel, and a bear."

"Coyotes. Owls! Do they eat those things?" asked Tamsen with a shudder.

Sam shrugged and said, "They are happy to get them. Their beef is all gone, unless they find some in the snow."

"Our beef cattle are all frozen, too, but I'm sure we have enough frozen meat to last a little while," said George.

"If we can find them in the snow. No telling where they wandered," said Jake.

Sam said, "When I left this morning a party of thirteen men and Mary Graves and Susan Foster were making backpacks. They are going to try to get over the divide."

"Stanton, too?" asked Elitha.

"And Mary Graves," said Leanna.

"Girls grow up," said George as he and Tamsen walked back to their shelter. Then he added with a chuckle, "I remember when my older girls first began to pay attention to boys."

Tamsen smiled. Yes, girls do grow up. The fleeting thought of the dozens of girls about this age whom she had known in her schoolwork was now overshadowed by the many problems at hand.

It froze that night. For nine days it alternately snowed, warmed a bit, froze, and again snowed.

Up to this time, with all their problems, Tamsen and Elizabeth had not been as worried about their meat supplies as the other emigrants had been, for they had a larger number of cattle. Even the loss of cattle to the Indians had not been catastrophic. This loss worried them. Men liked meat, and counting their teamsters and Elizabeth's two older boys, there were nine male appetites. The loss of milk for the children was the greatest concern. Their supply of flour was getting low even though it had been replenished when Stanton brought food on his mules.

Jean Baptiste went out with a long pole and plunged it deep into the snow. He could not find the frozen carcasses. The other hired men took turns getting wood and hunting for cattle, but they had no more luck than Baptiste.

The cut in George's hand began to fester. It crept up his arm. He was no longer able to cut wood nor help the men in their search for frozen cattle or for game. He did not make any trips to the lake for news, but sent in turn the hired men.

They learned that the party of thirteen men and two women who had planned to cross the divide on November 13 had to turn back before reaching the divide because the snow was soft and ten feet deep.

"Ten feet before the pass!" exclaimed Tamsen. "I wonder how deep it was at the pass."

About ten days of clear and warmer weather packed the snow. At night it froze and a crust formed. It would be easy traveling so George sent James Smith, who had formerly been a driver for Reed, up to the camp at the lake.

When he arrived he found that twenty-two persons, including six women at this time, were preparing to make another try at crossing the pass.

Early the next morning, November 21, the party including Stanton, with his six mules, and the two Indians started up the trail. James Smith could see that they actually got to the foot of the pass.

The next morning he was surprised to see everyone come stumbling back down. The mules could not travel the trail, for as soon as the air warmed up a bit their weight broke through the snow crust. Charles Stanton and his Indians refused to go on and leave their mules to die. They had promised Captain Sutter to return the mules. Only Stanton and the Indians knew the trail so the party returned to the lake.

James Smith returned to the Donners' shelters just

as a storm seemed to be forming.

After James Smith told the Donners about the experiences of those at the lake, Tamsen said, "It may be God's mercy that they returned. It looks as if we are in for a heavy snowstorm."

The next day was Thanksgiving, November 26. As much rain and sleet came down as snow, but by Saturday and Sunday the snow was heavy and began piling up over the shelters. The storm lasted until December 4.

Chapter 21

During the storm the Donners used the last of their meat supply. When the weather cleared they probed for cattle but none were found. Firewood, too, was hard to find. It was exhausting work for men weakened by malnutrition to collect wood and to cut it.

On December 9 came the third violent storm of the season. It lasted five days. Snow piled up higher on the shelters.

Death struck. Jake Donner died and then Sam Shoemaker. Both were victims of malnutrition.

On December 16, the second clear day after the storm, Tamsen sent Jean Baptiste to the lake to report Jake's and Sam's deaths. Jean learned that two men at the lake had also died, Milt Elliott and Baylis Williams.

He brought other news that was most intriguing. He said that a party of snowshoers had started for Sutter's mill. Elizabeth's older boys, Solomon and William Hook and Sonny Donner, listened eagerly to Jean's report.

"Snowshoes? What's that? How do they make them?" asked Solomon.

"Well you know the hickory bows that people use on the oxen. Mr. Graves sawed them into strips because they were too heavy. Then he took strips of ox hide and wove a surface between the strips of hickory."

"I bet we could make some like that," said Solomon. "I wish we had known about it. We could have gone with them."

"Oh, no, I need you. You are the only menfolks I have now," protested Elizabeth.

"Did Mr. Stanton go?" asked Elitha.

"Oh yes, and his Indians with him. Of course his mules are dead. They wandered away and died in the snow."

"Did Margaret Reed go?" asked Tamsen.

"No, she couldn't leave her children."

"Did Mary Graves go?" asked Leanna.

Elitha gave Leanna a nudge with her elbow. Tamsen was aware of this byplay.

"How many women went?" she asked.

"Seven women on snowshoes. Seven men had snowshoes. A couple of boys and a man thought they would go anyway, without snowshoes. But I wouldn't try it. I'm betting they come back after a day of it."

"How long do you suppose it will take? How about food?" asked George.

"They claimed they were taking enough for six days, but it sounded like skimpy rations: for each meal a stringy piece of dried beef about the size of my two fingers, a little coffee, and loaf sugar. Each one took a blanket or quilt, but the only clothes they had were what they were wearing."

Six days to Sutter's Fort, then hopefully rescuers would be sent for those left behind, thought Tamsen. Stanton, the rescuer was with them.

On nice days the Donners came out of their caves of snow, that is, all but George who was now confined to his bed. They breathed the clean mountain air and basked in the sunshine. Malnutrition was already taking its toll on the younger children. They did very little romping but played making sculptures in the snow.

James Smith and Noah James who had earlier gone up to the lake now came back to help Jean in his work. They hunted but could find no game. They had to go farther to look for wood.

The families began to use hides, the last contribution of the dead cattle and oxen they had been able to find. Elizabeth's boys worked with the women, singeing, then scraping the hair from the hides which were then thrown into the pot with the bones. The pots were kept at a simmer. When the hides were quite soft they yielded a kind of gelatinous soup. When cooled the mixture became gooey. The children called it glue.

Mrs. Wolfinger presided over the stew and made it somewhat palatable with herbs. Tamsen brought some epazote that she had picked when they had camped in moist grasslands. She found some mushrooms that she had picked when on the plains and offered them to other campers. But they were afraid to eat them, so now she had a nice pile of dried ones.

Mrs. Wolfinger seemed hesitant at first to use them.

Tamsen laughed and said, "You have to know which ones to pick. Our family ate plenty and they didn't kill us."

Mrs. Wolfinger nodded and said, *"Sehr gut."*

Tamsen added, "We do have some beans. The children will eat them if you season them with epazote."

Taking a basin of water and her medical kit, Tamsen went to George.

She said, "I'm sure Mrs. Wolfinger must have had a good education. She may have studied some English in school in Germany. Her German phrases come more easily to her. *Sehr gut.* Well it is *Sehr gut* for me to have her take over the cooking."

She began to unroll the bandages on George's arm. She frowned as she exposed the ugly area of infection which was creeping toward his elbow.

"Jake would not amputate it," said George. "I asked him about a week before he died to do it, but he would not."

Tamsen gasped. She was too horrified to make any

comment. She silently finished dressing his arm and climbed out of the shelter.

She walked over the snow, but she could not shake the fear that gripped her. A line of poetry came to mind from *Hamlet:* sicklied over with the pale cast of thought. No she must not deny it. She must let go and face the terrible truth--they might perish.

Acceptance of the truth brought her ease. She could go back to George now and face whatever the future brought them.

On the way back to the shelter, the tranquility, the sunshine, the sparkling snow, the shush sound of snow that slipped off the stretched-out limbs of the trees soothed her spirit. She noticed that these trees were unlike those in the east. When the snow fell off the branches here she saw that the branches were green. They had been green even through the storm.

She went back to the shelter. As she entered she heard Eliza exclaim, "Oh, chicken," as she fished out bits of food floating in the bowl of soup that Mrs. Wolfinger had given her.

Tamsen was startled. Of course, it couldn't be chicken. Back home rabbit would sometimes be served, and the children would mistake it for chicken. They had often had fowl on the trip, but she had not heard any rifle shot this morning. If Jean Baptiste had shot a wild duck, he would have been excited and shown his prize to everybody. Now he was holding a whispered conversation with Mrs. Wolfinger and both were avoiding her eyes.

Suddenly Tamsen guessed. There were just some things people did not eat.

George said from his bed, "Something the matter?"

She went to him and said, "I don't know what animal she has put in the pot. I think it is something Jean brought her."

George spoke calmly, "There are all kinds of game in different parts of the world. You'd eat bear meat, wouldn't you? You learned to eat buffalo meat last summer, didn't you?"

"Some things are just varmints or rodents," protested Tamsen.

"What is a varmint for one may be game for another person," said George.

The children seemed satisfied and happy. Tamsen could not touch the food that day, but by the next day she took a bowl of the soup. A person must survive. Most important they must see to it that the children survived. Even animals put survival of their young before their own.

Chapter 22

On December 22 Tamsen said, "The snowshoers left on December sixteenth. They thought it would take six days. That's today. They should be at Sutter's."

"Let's hope so," said George. "They took rations for only six days.They should be starting back soon with food. Maybe Sutter will send mules again."

George then turned to the subject of Christmas. "I hope Jean finds some kind of game so we can have a feast. He said he knew where a bear was hibernating."

Tamsen said, "I asked him to get us a small pine. The girls can decorate it. We can give each girl a book."

"I'm sorry about your school supplies," said George, patting her with his good hand.

"Oh, I'll give them one of my own books that I have here in the wagon. I'll give Eliza a *McDuffy Reader*. She can read most of it already. Georgia can have the fairy-tale book, and Frances can have Hawthorne's *Twice Told Tales*. Leanna would like any book by Sir Walter Scott and Elitha would like Lamb's *Tales from Shakespeare*. Of course they have read most of the books, but they will be owning them. We can spare a little sugar for treats."

The next morning the fourth storm of the season broke. It raged its fury for two days. It calmed down on Christmas enough for Elizabeth's children to come to see the tree gaily decorated with angels and chains made of paper. Tamsen saved back some sugar and each child was given a lump. The girls enjoyed their books.

December 26 was a clear day. Now surely, thought Tamsen, the storms were over. The fifth storm came on January 9 and lasted four days, the sixth on January 22. It lasted five days.

The rhythm of the weather patterned their lives to the confinement in their shelters during the storms and enjoyment of the outdoors during the clear weather. The fresh air was a tonic. The pines silhouetted against the white hills enticed Tamsen to bring out her easel and canvas. She tried to catch the translucence of the snow and the subtle shadows of the green. The scene needed a broader canvas than the dainty pictures she had painted for her book.

She used her last piece of canvas and then went down the steps of the shelter to give it to George.

George was too ill to climb the steps up out of the shelter.

Tamsen said, "It's like a sea of pines out there."

"Sea of pines," said George. "My little professor sounds poetic."

"Yes, it is poetry but not mine. It is a phrase from a hymn by Samuel Taylor Colderidge."

"A hymn? I don't think I ever heard it."

"Probably not. I don't think it would be in the hymnbook of the German Reformed Church."

"Everybody in our church speaks English. Why do they call it German?" asked Frances.

"A lot of early settlers were from Germany."

George went on to tell the girls about the first Donners who had come from Germany, and other family tales.

Tamsen realized from the day George had talked about amputation that he was trying to come to grips with the possibility of death. She herself had faced the possibility that afternoon. It seemed they had to face it separately. Then their conversation flowed in mutual understanding as they tried to ease each other's pain and shield the girls from their fear. George often made comments in appreciation of Tamsen's literary and artistic abilities. He recalled the pleasures of the winter evenings back in Illinois when his neighbors gathered at their home to listen to Tamsen read.

During the storms the girls sat on their beds and read, first their own books and then each other's. During the heaviest of the storms the light was dim so Tamsen recited poetry from the Bible stories she knew almost by heart. Their candles were all used up and they had to burn pine cones for light.

She read aloud to George. He especially enjoyed Dicken's *Pickwick Papers* and Edgar Allen Poe's mysteries. Among the books stacked on top of a packing case was the one that George and Jake had pored over last winter before they left Illinois, *The Emigrant's Guide to Oregon and California* by Lansford Warren Hastings. There was a passage that George had underlined and had shown frequently to anyone who would listen. As Tamsen was stacking the books in order, the pages flipped open to the marked passage describing California:

Even in the months of
December and January vegetation is
in full bloom and all nature wears
a most cheerful and enlivening
aspect. It may truly be said
December is as pleasant as May.

The remarks made here in
reference to the mildness and
uniformity of the climate are
applicable only to the valleys and
plains, the mountains present one
eternal winter.

She handed the book to George without comment.

He read it silently.

On the trail, when anything went wrong, the tendency was to blame Lansford Hastings. Yet Mr. Hastings had apparently brought his party to the land where nature wears a most cheerful and enlivening aspect. Did the fault lie with any one person? Stanton had pointed out that their lack of cooperation could lead to disaster. Probably he had been right. As farmers they were used to disasters caused by nature, such as drought, cyclones, infestations, floods, and freezes. There would be only one thing to do: go ahead with the work and have faith that the next time things would go better. This was their individual virtue. But they often lacked cooperation with others in the same situation.

Later George said, "You can't blame one man for what has happened. Nature, especially weather, can work havoc."

"Yes. As Burns said: The best laid schemes o' mice and men gang aft a-gley," said Tamsen.

Chapter 23

The book around which there was the most discussion was *The Taming of the Shrew* in Lamb's *Tales From Shakespeare*. Elitha read it first and then asked Tamsen to read it aloud.

Tamsen said, "I wish I had my Shakespeare copy. When I was in school our drama class put on the play. I was Kate."

"I wouldn't want to be Kate," said Elitha with spirit. "I don't like--I mean, to have to obey Petruchio."

"I like Bianco, but I don't like the way her father wouldn't let her marry until Kate did," said Leanna.

Tamsen smiled at the seriousness of the girls' expressions. She glanced at George who lifted his eyebrows and nodded.

"I'm going to be a teacher and get married, too," said Elitha.

Mrs. Wolfinger was listening. There was a brief eye-to-eye exchange between her and Tamsen and then addressing the girls she said, "Feminists."

Tamsen was surprised. Did Mrs. Wolfinger mean it as approval?

"What does feminist mean?" asked Leanna.

"Mrs. Breen called Mamma a fem--a femin something," said Frances.

"Big ears," said Leanna. "You shouldn't be listening all the time."

"It means that women want equal rights, those that men have. They want jobs such as men have. Teaching."

"Didn't you teach?" asked Frances.

"Yes, I taught in Newburyport, Massachusetts, right after I graduated," said Tamsen.

"I thought you taught in North Carolina," said

Elitha.

"Yes, I did for quite a number of years. I studied there, too."

"I read about a girl named Susan Anthony. She started teaching when she was fifteen years old. They said she was a feminist."

"That is because she is active in the Temperance Society," said Tamsen. "Some women, like Julia Ward Howe write about abolition. Lucretia Mott and Elizabeth Cady Stanton lecture for women's rights to own property, to have a college education, and even to vote. They are all called feminists."

Leanna said, "I read about Belva Ann Bennett. She started teaching when she was fourteen, but they would not pay her as much as they paid the man teacher. She got only five dollars a month with room and board. Then she found the man got ten dollars. That made her mad. She complained to the trustees. That's why it got in the papers. But I didn't read what happened. They said she was growing up to be a feminist."

"I'm almost fifteen," said Elitha, "and I could start teaching."

"Maybe in a country school, but it is better to have more education. Now they are starting schools for women. There's Mt. Holyoke for women and Oberlin College for both women and men."

"Did you go to college?" asked Frances.

"In my day, when young women finished the local school they went to academies or finishing schools."

"Were you a feminist?"

Tamsen noticed that they had asked *were* not *are*. She answered, "I never thought of myself as one. I was myself doing what I wanted to do. Yet I think women should be allowed to be doctors, lawyers, or what they want to be and should be allowed to study courses they want, but I haven't written or agitated about it."

"You write for the *Springfield Journal*," said Frances, who was learning to write. It seemed to be of great importance to her.

"How do you know they will print that letter you gave to the scout when we were on the prairie?"

George said, "If the scout delivers it, Editor Allen Francis will publish it all right. He asked your mother to write about the trip."

"I read that some feminists believe that women should have the right to vote."

"The right to vote! That would be wonderful," said Tamsen. "But all men can't vote yet. Even free negroes can't in most free states."

"Then you are a feminist," said Leanna.

"You are not," said Frances decisively, "You're a mamma."

"What do you know? You aren't seven yet," said Leanna.

Later as George lay on his blankets and the girls were out getting some fresh air, he said to Tamsen, "I'm really getting acquainted with my daughters. The things they chatter about. I think we should teach them to say that they are the children of Mr. and Mrs. George Donner. Just in case."

Tamsen realized that this was another step in his coming to grips with death. But neither could put that thought into words. She said, "In case we get separated."

"Yes," said George. "Eliza will speak up easily. She will probably proclaim her name and age. But Georgia is rather shy. Also Leanna and Elitha were asking about their own mother. I told them to talk to their Aunt Elizabeth about her. You know their mother and their

Aunt Elizabeth were sisters."

"Yes, and you should tell the girls more about yourself."

That's a stark admission of why we are saying this, thought Tamsen. George seemed to understand.

"Yes, they need to know about the Donners in North Carolina, Kentucky, and Indiana. To them Illinois is the center of the world."

The *Springfield Journal* and other newspapers had been crushed and used for packing in the many drawers, boxes, and barrels. As supplies were used the crumpled papers were spread out and interesting bits of news would cause the girls as much excitement as a new paper.

They knew their father was interested in public affairs in Springfield, particularly in a candidate named Abraham Lincoln who was running for the legislature.

"Yes, I read this about a year ago," said George when the girls pointed out the news item. "I wonder if he won. Did you know, Tamsen, that James Reed served under Abe Lincoln in the Mohawk wars?"

Tamsen nodded and glanced up from the item the girls had given her about Lucretia Mott, the Quaker preacher. With such scraps of information they kept in touch with the outer world as it had been.

Chapter 24

The seventh storm of the season which began on February 2 was not the howling blizzard of the earlier storms, but a gentle falling of snow. It continued for five days, the fluffy white mounds piling high over the packed snows of previous storms.

The Donner families each stayed in their own shelters. Jean Baptiste and Noah James were in the tepee. On the afternoon of the second day Jean Baptiste came to the Donner shelter.

"Noah is awfully sick. Have you any medicine?" he asked.

Tamsen gathered together a few medicines and with Jean climbed up out of the shelter. Fairly firm steps had been made out of the packed snow of earlier storms, but this new snow was soft and did not hold their weight.

Jean went on ahead, his legs cutting a swath in the new-fallen snow. Tamsen, who was short and encumbered by a long skirt, found each step beyond her stride. Jean gradually got farther ahead of her. The falling snow was a curtain and soon she could not see him.

She realized that she was no longer following in his steps. She became panicky. She was exhausted. She had to stop a moment to catch her breath. She hugged her box of medicines under her shawl.

After a pause she tried to take the next step, but now she seemed to be deeper in the snow. She had to lay the box aside and scoop the barrier of snow away. She struggled step by step, picking up the box, taking a step, and laying down the box while she scooped more snow.

She had to rest. The falling snow was a soft blanket. She began to get drowsy. She would rest just a little bit more. The blanket was so cozy--she ought to start--just a little more rest. Drowsy--drifting-- the falling snow covered her box.

A voice was calling, or was it a voice? She was floating, tranquil. She knew she must arouse herself but she seemed to slide away.

She was roughly grabbed by the shoulders as Jean remonstrated, "You didn't stay in my tracks. You went the wrong way. The tepee is over this way."

Jean picked up the box, and half-dragging Tamsen, he steered her to the teepee.

There was only the warmth and the light of a few pine cones, but there was a job for Tamsen to do. She sat up with her patient most of the night, until he seemed better. He was breathing more easily.

Jean accompanied her back to George.

"I know where a bear is hibernating," said Jean who liked to have George entrust him with his guns.

Tamsen said, "There is only one hide left. Mrs. Wolfinger and I will have to scrape that today, so I hope you do get some game. The bean sacks are empty. I put some water in the crocks that had the sugar. It will be sweet from the residue."

George said, "Go try to get something, Jean. But I think you had better probe some more for the cattle. I know there are a number out there somewhere and you have to find them soon while they are frozen. By the time the snow melts all around them the meat will be rotten."

Tamsen said, "Not having milk is the worst. The girls can't stomach the broth from the hides. That broth is the one thing that keeps me going. I'm afraid the girls will starve if Jean doesn't find something soon."

Elizabeth was ill and Tamsen went over to see her. Her three little boys sat around listlessly and had to be urged to go out in the sun. Mary and nine-year-old George (often called Sonny to distinguish him from Uncle George) were weak from hunger but were able to wait on their mother and their younger brothers. The Hook boys were out hunting for wood.

Elizabeth, on the verge of tears, said, "I just won't. I'd rather die than do it."

"Do what?" asked Tamsen in alarm.

"Don't you know?"

"Know what?" asked Tamsen, fearing that she should have guessed. "The bodies?"

"Yes, Jean he--" She shuddered. "First Sam's body. But the children are dying of starvation. I couldn't myself, but I couldn't say no to the children. Now he has uncovered Jake's body. I can't, but the children--"

Tamsen was too shocked to comfort Elizabeth. She returned to her own shelter unable to hide her distress.

When George saw her face he asked what happened.

Her words stumbled, "Elizabeth says Jean . . . well, the bodies . . . it is just cannibalism!"

George, too, was distressed. He said, "William and Solomon Hook came to me about it. They were desperate, and at first their mother would not consent, but with seven children starving, what could one do. Jean was a desert waif and has probably eaten human flesh before. After all, we believe that the person no longer inhabits the body. Tell Elizabeth I'm sure Jake would be willing, and glad to be able to save his children." Then he added bitterly, "With this stinking arm I couldn't even do that for my children. I'd be poison. We must do everything possible for their survival. Besides I doubt that they realize what is happening."

"Maybe Frances does," said Tamsen. "The others call her big ears. I call her big eyes. Sunday she asked me why I didn't eat something from a certain pot. I told her it looked as if the girls had eaten it all."

"I noticed," said George, "that Mrs. Wolfinger had been serving the girls something surreptitiously, but I don't know whether she ate it. I have no appetite, though I force myself to take a little broth from that concoction of bones and hides. It is not pleasant but I can tolerate it. The girls must survive."

Tamsen said, "It makes me angry that Jean did not consult me. He consulted Elizabeth."

"Jean respects you," said George. "That was really a tribute to you."

Tribute? What does he mean?

George was dropping off to sleep and Tamsen left the shelter. Beyond the shelter, up an incline, was a tree that was at her favorite place for meditation. Her anger still burned against Jean. Then as it subsided, she leaned against the tree and buried her face in her hands and cried. The thought of her girls' lost innocence was unbearable. They had eaten human flesh. Finally she was able to accept it with a fierce determination that they must survive.

What had George meant by saying it was a tribute? Then it came to her, *Jean knew she would not eat human flesh*. That was a tribute to her steadfastness. But as to the children--they must survive.

For a few days it was pleasant spring weather. The girls escaped the fetid air of the shelters and sat on blankets on the snow. They sat listlessly. There was no romping and no building of sculptures.

Tamsen heard their occasional bits of conversation.

"Mr. Reed has a family. Mr. Stanton said he got to Sutter's Fort."

"Mr. McCutchen, too. He'll come back for his baby."

"All those people went on snowshoes. They'll tell

Capt'n Sutter."

Though now Tamsen and George had together faced the probability that they themselves might not survive, they encouraged themselves with every sign of spring and speculated continually about what those who had crossed over the mountain would now be doing. James Reed would certainly come to the rescue of his family. Also there was William McCutchen and fourteen snowshoers already there, most of them with families who needed to be rescued. The weather kept nice. Might they not come by February 17 or by February 18. Each day they could bolster hope for just one more day.

Chapter 25

On February 19 at about ten o'clock Elizabeth's three little boys were seated on tree stumps, their starved bodies hunched over. Noah James had gone looking for game. Jean and the Hook boys were dragging a felled tree when they spied three men coming down the trail.

Jean shouted, "Mrs. Donner. Mrs. Donner. They're coming. They're coming!"

The little boys paid no attention. Mary and Sonny hurried up out of Elizabeth's shelter. Solomon Hook dashed down to help his mother come up.

Tamsen and Mrs. Wolfinger came out of their shelter. They watched as the three bearded men came down the trail and stopped first at Elizabeth's place.

The men opened their sacks and distributed jerked beef. Mary and the older boys chewed it, but they had to coax the little boys to even taste it. Elizabeth sent William inside for a crock. One man opened a sack and poured some course ground flour into the crock.

Then the men came over to the George Donner shelter. By this time all the girls had joined Tamsen. The men distributed the jerked beef and everyone began munching.

One man handed the sack of flour, now only half full, to Mrs. Wolfinger, who hurried down to make pancakes.

Tamsen said, "Thank God. You are angels from heaven."

"I'm Reasin Tucker," said the older man, "and this here is Sept Moultry, and over there John Rhoads. We come over with Glover's gang. Seven of us. Glover stayed at the lake with three other fellows. Them folks up there are just all starving. They're feeding them up so we can get started back to Fort Sutter. Glover says to take only those who can walk."

"Come see my husband."

Tucker accompanied Tamsen to George's bedside. Mrs. Wolfinger went back up with a plate of pancakes.

Tamsen said, "George needs to get to a doctor. Did you bring a wagon?"

"No, lady. That's impossible. Horses and mules can't get through the deep snow. Seven of us got here with only backpacks. I'll report to Woodworth at Mule Springs and he can see what can be done after the snow melts. It will probably freeze over tonight, so we better leave early tomorrow morning before the warm sun makes mush out of the trail. We are to take only those who can walk."

They continued the discussion and it was decided that Mrs. Wolfinger and Elitha could go. Leanna, who had been ill, revived as soon as she had some food. She could also go. Elizabeth said she needed to have Solomon stay with her. But she would let George (Sonny) and William go.

"Both Noah James and Jean Baptiste want to go, too," said Moultry.

"No," said Tucker, "both can't go. Glover said to leave one to look after the sick. Noah has been ill so Jean will have to stay."

Jean ranted and raved, but George promised to make it worth his while to stay.

Since the three men were staying overnight, Mrs. Wolfinger baked more biscuits. There was now very little flour or beef left for those who would not be going.

The men had the evening to tell of their experiences after being hired to join the crew of rescuers. On January 31 they started with Glover. He had a pack train of horses and mules with supplies collected at Sutter's Fort. From there they went to Johnson's Ranch where they slaughtered cattle, cut the meat into strips, and dried it out over fires. Johnson had no mill. They pounded the wheat and ground it in coffee mills.

Fourteen men with horses and pack mules loaded with supplies left Johnson's Ranch February four. It rained for twenty-four hours and then snowed. At Mule Springs the snow was so deep the horses and mules could go no farther. They made camp and left Woodworth in charge of supplies. They sent the mules and horses back to the ranch with Eddy and another young fellow.

"Eddy!" exclaimed Tamsen. "Do you know him?"

"Yes. He's a brave young fellow. Two weeks before he was practically a goner, but he insisted on joining up."

Tamsen was aghast. "He was with the snowshoers. When did he arrive?"

"January seventeenth he got to Johnson's Ranch, more dead than alive."

"They left December sixteenth. That's over a month! They had food for only six days. They must have starved, unless Eddy got some game."

"I heard he shot only one deer," said John Rhoads.

"What did they do for food?"

There was dead silence. The men exchanged significant glances. Jean and Mrs. Wolfinger sat tight-lipped. Tamsen looked at George. His eyes told her that he, too, guessed the unspoken answer: cannibalism.

George turned the conversation. "Did you hear anything about Charles Stanton?"

All three shook their heads.

"The name Woodworth sounds familiar, but I can't place him," said Tamsen.

John Rhoads grinned and began to hum a tune.

"*The Old Oaken Bucket* by Samuel Woodworth," said George and Tamsen together.

"Do you know anything about James Reed? I heard he got to Sutter's Fort all right."

"Sure, ma'am. Everybody has heard about him. He's the one that made all the speeches about the emigrants getting caught in the snow. His own family, too. He was so choked up telling about it that Reverend Dunlevy got up and made a speech and they took up a collection. He got thirteen hundred dollars, they say, at San Jose. He is the fellow who bought supplies and shipped them up the Sacramento River. A man named McCutchen bought mules and horses, all the stuff that Woodworth has now at Mule Springs."

The next morning the three men accompanied by William Hook, George (Sonny) Donner, Elitha, Leanna, Noah James, and Mrs. Wolfinger started for the lake.

Tucker's final word was, "Woodworth should be along very soon with men and supplies."

Tamsen's little girls, especially Frances, seemed quite concerned about the departure of Leanna and Elitha.

Frances said, "Just the big children could go, couldn't they."

"Yes, just the big children because the little children have to be carried. Mr. Tucker said more men would come and help carry the little ones."

Georgia said, "The man told me that the snow was so deep that it was way up over the packhorses." She raised her arms as far as she could and added, "Leanna and Elitha are so big. They aren't as big as the horses."

"The men have to cut trails for the people to walk on," said Tamsen. "Then they will come and get us."

In assuring her girls, Tamsen was trying to assure herself.

Tucker's men had cut some wood for them so Jean was free to look for game. They heard geese honking, but Jean had come back empty-handed.

Tamsen said, "I can stretch this beef and flour to last three or maybe four days. I do have a small piece of hide left, but the girls can't eat that. Let's hope Reed or Woodworth gets here soon."

George said, "Tucker told me they were taking the Reed family with them, so there is no real need for Reed to come all this way. Reed has already done a big job raising money and hauling supplies to the base camp that Woodworth has set up at Mule Springs. Besides food for us they have to haul in enough to feed the men at Mule Springs. Even if the mules get only that far, they have to be fed."

George was always was careful of stock, thought Tamsen. She said, "We should be thankful for the wonderful people in California. It's a miracle the way they have given money and have rallied to organize a company of men to rescue us."

In her thoughts Tamsen hoped for another miracle: that as soon as the snow melted Woodworth would send a horse and wagon to take George.

The meager rations were stretched five days, but no one came.

February 25, February 26, February 27, and February 28 passed, but no one came.

Sharp-eyed Frances seemed to be aware that her parents and Aunt Elizabeth did not eat certain things that Jean prepared.

Chapter 26

Tamsen sat by George sponging his arm. The fire was burning in the pit, keeping warm the last bit of broth that had been extracted from the last piece of hide. Thinned and seasoned it was somewhat palatable but not sustaining. George had no appetite. The children were nauseated by the broth. Tamsen had hoped she would not again have to use flesh.

The warmth of the morning air had softened the crust of frozen snow so that Jean's boots sounded *slush, slush* as he came down the steps.

Tamsen asked hopefully, "Did you find any game?"

"No, mum, but here's some flour. There's two men from the lake camp over at the other cabin. They are trying to get the little ones to eat some jerky. The missis is too sick to bake anything. She said to bring the flour to you."

As he talked Tamsen rounded up her utensils and set out her soda and cream of tarter to make biscuits.

"Woodworth's men I suppose?"

"They didn't say. They said there were eight men at the lake getting people ready to go, and some would come tomorrow to take us. You bet I'm going this time," he said defiantly.

The next morning James Reed arrived with three men.

Tamsen greeted him enthusiastically. "We scarcely expected you, but I am so glad. We heard that Glover was taking your family and that Woodworth would be coming. How are Margaret and the children?"

"Glover did start out with them but on the second day Tommy got completely petered out. Glover took him back to the lake and Patti went with him. They stayed with the Breens. But the refugees had a difficult time. Glover had cached some food in a tree, but animals climbed the tree and got all the food. The refugees were without food for five days. Glover went ahead to Mule Springs to get some provisions. I met him, and when I heard they were out of food I stayed up most of the night and baked bread and made sweet cakes. The next morning I met them. Margaret had collapsed in the snow. Virginia was barely able to stagger to meet me. They will be all right now. I left plenty of food until they get to Mule Springs."

"Elitha and Leanna? Are they all right?"

"They will be. They were exhausted like the rest, but with food they perked up. Don't worry about them anymore. There's supplies at Mule Springs. Also Captain Kern is establishing a relay camp of supplies. There's supplies at Johnson's Ranch and a few more miles there is Sutter's Fort."

"How wonderful the California people have been to us!" exclaimed Tamsen.

"Yes, Alcolade Bartlett and Governor Hull are backing up the relief work with money and necessities."

Tamsen asked hopefully, "Do you suppose they would be able to bring horses and a wagon for George? You come on down and see him."

Tamsen took Reed to George who was in bed. She knew Reed was shocked to see him in such a weakened state. George was unable to talk very much, but he was an attentive listener.

Reed told him of his experiences since reaching Sutter's Fort. He had bought supplies last November. He and McCutchen had started from Johnson's Ranch with mules loaded with packs of food, but the snow was too deep for the mules. Then he and McCutchen backpacked part of the supplies until they, too, were bogged down in the snow just the other side of the pass. He told of his efforts to get capable men interested, and of his stint in Fremont's army. He was an officer and was recruiting for Fremont. He praised such men as Glover, Tucker, and the men who were with him, including McCutchen and Hiram Miller, their friend from Springfield.

George said "Springfield. Any news of last fall's election?"

"Oh, yes. Papers come to San Francisco by ship. I read that Abe Lincoln won. He's now a member of Congress."

George smiled but seemed overly tired, so Tamsen and Reed went outside to talk.

"Did Stanton get through with the snowshoers all right?" asked Tamsen.

Reed hesitated and said sadly, "Only two men of the snowshoers got through. All the women survived. Stanton suffered from snow blindness. By the sixth day he was utterly exhausted. The whole group rested and when they were ready to leave Mary Graves asked him if he were coming. He said he would be along in a little while but he never joined them. Then came that terrible snowstorm we had just before Christmas."

Then he died in the snow. How beautiful," said Tamsen.

Reed was shocked. "Tamsen Donner, how can you say that. There have been many tragic deaths."

"Yes, but dying in a snowstorm is not tragic. It is like being wrapped in a cloud and going to sleep."

Reed looked at her strangely. She sensed that he wondered what her experience had been, but she would not share that. There had been something mystical and sacred about it.

She said, "I was reading a book by a doctor who

wrote that victims of exposure often cease to feel cold. Instead they drift first into a phase of relaxed contentment and thence into sleep. Our party has had so many tragic deaths."

"So many little children have died," said Reed sadly.

"How about getting a wagon for George?" asked Tamsen.

Reed shook his head sadly. "You realize, don't you, that George is very close to death? We could not get a wagon over the pass. Neither horses nor mules can get through those drifts. Even if we could bring a doctor to him tomorrow, it would be too late."

In her heart Tamsen had known and accepted it. She knew George had accepted it, too, but still she held on to hope.

Reed said, "I had hoped to be able to take everybody, but I'll have to leave some. Woodworth will be along soon. I'll take the Breens. The situation is pretty bad at the Murphy cabin. I'll have to leave ten-year-old Simon to look after his mother. Mrs. Murphy is too ill to travel. She has been trying to take care of her little grandson and little Jimmy Eddy, but the two little fellows are awfully sick, maybe dying. Also I'll have to leave Keseberg, who has a crippled foot. That's five I'm leaving at the lake."

"Are you taking Eleanor Eddy?"

"She and her little girl died a short time ago. I think Eddy will come with Woodworth. I hope little Jimmy lives until his father gets to him. Now I must go over to Elizabeth's and see what arrangements I can make for her family. You get yourself and the girls ready to go."

When Tamsen went again to George's bedside he

said, "You and the girls must go with Reed. I'm not long for this world. Reed said he would leave a couple of his men to look after me."

"I can't leave you," said Tamsen, bending over and putting her cheek against his.

Reed came back from the other shelter and said, "Elizabeth is too ill to travel and also her two little boys are very sick. I think Isaac could go. He is six and Solomon could look after him. I'll take Mary. I'll leave someone to help Jean look after the others."

"Jean was promised that he could go this time," said Tamsen. "He won't be very happy about being left."

"I've made a deal with him, and he is willing to stay, I'll leave Clark to care for George, and Cady and Stone can help out at either camp when needed."

"But I am not going," said Tamsen. "Can you take the girls?"

"You must go. The girls will need to be carried part of the time. I don't have enough men. I anticipate having to carry Tommy much of the way."

"Yes, you go," said George.

"There, listen to your husband. You are the lady with the New England conscience. You promised to obey your husband."

"My New England conscience? I've heard that before. But remember the vows are also till death do us part. I'm staying."

"Well, Woodworth will be along in a few days. I can leave enough food for a week."

Tamsen went over to Elizabeth's to help her get her children ready for the trip, and left Reed for his final parting with George.

The three little girls stood by her side as Reed and their cousins went up the trail.

Frances said, "Mary is going. She is eight years old, and I am almost eight. Nobody would have to carry me."

Watching until the party was out of sight the girls waved and said, "Good-bye. Good-bye. Good-bye."

Chapter 27

After James Reed and the children left, Tamsen walked away from the shelters to a spot where the snow lay unsullied, away from the debris scattered around and now beginning to show in the untidy slush of the melting snow. The pines stood silent sentinels. The sun was warm.

New England conscience, thought Tamsen. What do people mean by that? A straitjacket? When she first went to North Carolina friends teased her, using the same expression. She sensed what they meant, for they had an acceptance of things as they happened that she grew to appreciate. Those had been happy years, studying, and finding success in teaching. Then a happy marriage ending in tragedy. After the deaths in her family she had gone back to Massachusetts. That New England conscience, whatever it meant, was a bulwark in death, an acceptance of God's will. Her brother's family, her neighbors, the church, made the climate in which she had to grow and go on living.

No, James Reed did not understand. It was not the straitjacket of her New England conscience that kept her at George's side. It was her feeling that her marriage to George was something special, though in a way not always expected in second marriages. She had not entered this marriage with romantic expectations. Widows and spinster schoolteachers had no status. It was expected that a widow would remarry.

In the years she had been married to George there had grown a bond of commitment between them. There had been give-and-take, even on this trip. She had not wanted to come by the Salt Lake route, but once the decision was made she had wholeheartedly stood by George.

It's the suffering element
that measures love.

That quotation from Henry Ward Beecher's sermon had stayed with her. They had suffered together and that suffering had indeed bound them more closely.

She heard giggles and shouts from the little girls. She saw that Jean had taken them to a high spot beyond the shelter where the snow was cleaner. The girls were on a piece of canvas and Jean pulled them up and down the slope.

She went to George. He was in a fitful sleep. She thought of that night when he had said, "We are together." She knew he was offering her the pearl of great price. In her mind she answered James Reed: *If you had accepted something of great value then the honorable thing is to pay the price.*

The next two days the weather was fine. There was a little food, hopefully enough to last a few days until Woodworth would arrive. Jean again went probing for frozen beef. If any could be found it must be found right away for soon the weather would spoil it. Clark saw a mother bear and her cub. He shot and wounded the bear and was following the trail of blood. Reed had left Stone on duty at the lake camp and had left Cady to care for Elizabeth and the two sick little boys, Sammy and Lewis.

Tamsen went to see Elizabeth and the little boys. Cady said his patients were sleeping, so she left.

George, too, was sleeping.

Tamsen and the girls spread a blanket on the snow. Tamsen read stories from the Bible. The girls chanted verses they had learned. In unison they chanted, "We are the children of Mr. and Mrs. George Donner."

"Is Papa going to die?" asked Frances suddenly.

Tamsen was startled. Where had Big Ears got that?

Though she herself knew it in her heart, nothing had been said except her conversation with James Reed. Of course the girls realized that their cousin Mary's father, Uncle Jake had died. Georgia and Eliza looked at their mother in distress. She had thought that she had shielded them.

"Where would we go? Would we die, too?"

Tamsen was disturbed. To this moment she had not questioned her choice, her duty. She got up and walked agitatedly over to the road that led to the lake. Would Woodworth come soon?

She saw a man coming down the trail. Was it Woodworth? No, it was Stone whom Reed had left at the lake camp. He slipped into Elizabeth's shelter to talk to Cady.

Soon Cady and Stone approached her smiling and suggested that they take her little girls on Reed's trail. They could carry them when they couldn't walk. They could catch up with Reed's party. He must be barely over the pass, for last night Stone had seen his campfire on this side of the pass.

Then they began bargaining. They would take the girls for five hundred dollars.

Was that right? What was her duty? It was a hard choice. Must the hard choice always be the right choice?

The girls came from the blanket and stood beside her and searched her face. They seemed to have no fear, probably because their stepsisters and cousin Mary had already gone. Their remark about death still troubled her. Wasn't her first duty to them to see that they survived? She had already violated her code for the purpose of their survival. Who would take care of them? In California they would have sisters, and friends. The people had been so wonderful.

She said, "Yes. But I can't send them looking like

ragamuffins. Give me a half an hour."

Tamsen combed their hair, dressed them in quilted petticoats, linsey dresses, and woolen stockings. Georgia and Eliza wore knitted red hoods and garnet red twill cloaks. Frances had a blue hood and a warm shawl.

Tamsen decided to send some of her small pieces of silver and her expensive silks and satins. The fabrics would not be so very heavy and the silver could be sold to help care for the children. She lay each piece with loving care in the sack and on top she put the girls' best party dresses, dove-colored for Frances, light brown for Georgia, and dark brown for Eliza.

She took the girls to George's bedside for their last good-byes. The feeling which she had been able to ignore while busy with the dressing of the girls swept over her. Was this really her duty? The young men were waiting on the steps, and she led the girls to them.

She kissed the girls, and as though speaking in a daze to herself and to God, she said, "God will take care of you. Dear God--"

They were gone, trudging through the snow. She saw that Eliza soon had to be carried.

The pain of departure settled into an acceptance, but there was a small nagging kernel of doubt left. She tried to reason it away. They were only twenty-four hours behind Reed's party and they would soon catch up with him. The weather was clear. It was a beautiful spring day.

She went to sit by George's bedside. He seemed only half-aware of the departure of the little girls.

That night in her diary she did not express her doubts, but clung to her faith that she had done the right thing. She filled the page with notes about the girls; little things she wanted to remember.

The last line was a prayer.

Chapter 28

March 6, the second day after the girls' departure, the eighth storm of the season swept with hurricane force around the peaks and into the valleys. Tamsen, in addition to her worry about the girls, felt disoriented. She no longer had the assurance of rightness which usually followed her decisions. Had her decision been wrong? No. As far as staying with George was concerned it was the right one. As to letting the girls go? Her belief in herself was eroding. Mr. Reed had said she had a New England conscience. Maybe she did, but it had always provided her with a rod to lean on.

The storm lasted three nights and two days. Tamsen was alone with George in her shelter. Clark had failed to catch the bear, and only a little flour was left. The wood supply gave out and both shelters were cold. Elizabeth's little boy Lewis died the second night of the storm. Elizabeth was frantic with grief and that night she died in her sleep. Sammy seemed at the point of death. Tamsen took him and laid him in the bed beside George.

When the storm cleared Jean and Clark went hunting, and Clark soon found the bear he had been tracking. Tamsen then sent him to the lake to learn what he could about another rescue party coming.

Returning, Clark said, "Ma'am, the three little girls are there in the Murphy cabin. There's just Mrs. Murphy, her kid Simon, and the old crazy kook, Keseberg."

"Where are Cady and Stone?"

"Oh, they skedaddled with the loot and dropped the girls off at the cabin."

Tamsen left Clark to care for George and started for the lake, carrying a basket with a few biscuits.

Tamsen's thoughts were simply: Thank God they

were alive. Thank God they were alive.

The trail from Alder Creek to the lake was soggy with melting snow. Tamsen was exhausted and stumbled in a heap as she reached the door of the Murphy cabin.

Ten-year-old Simon Murphy was rubbing off in the snow the charred hairs of a piece of hide, and was eating the crisped pieces. The boy helped Tamsen into the cabin.

The air was foul, still smelling of the singeing of the hide rug, a small fragment of which remained on the floor.

When Simon opened the door a man in one corner raised his head and shouted and mumbled a mixture of curses and unintelligible syllables. Mrs. Murphy lay moaning in bed.

Hearing someone come in, she raised her head and screamed, "He killed him. He killed my baby. Georgie, my baby. He killed little Jimmie, too."

Tamsen seemed almost paralyzed for a moment. Her eyes searched frantically for her girls. In the corner farthest from the fire which suddenly flared up from some wood Simon threw on it, she saw a bundle of dirty blankets in motion. Three heads popped up.

"Mamma. Mamma," Eliza cried out.

The man raised his head and screamed at her to shut up. She subsided into convulsive sobs. Glancing at Tamsen, the man lay back and began to mumble again.

Tamsen took Eliza into her arms and the other two crawled out of the blankets and crowded close to her side. She noticed that their bed had been just a pile of branches. Choking in the foul air she led the girls outside.

She seated them on a pile of firewood, gave them each a biscuit, and listened to the story they had to tell.

Frances said, "I don't think the man killed Georgie. He was awfully sick and he was cold and Mrs. Murphy put him in the man's bed to get him warm."

"Georgie was Mrs. Murphy's grandson, wasn't he? Sarah and William Foster must have left him with her when they went on snowshoes. I thought Eddy's little boy Jimmie was here, too."

"Uh-uh. He cried and cried and he just died. Simon said his mamma and his baby sister died, too, but that was before we came here," said Frances.

"Poor Eddy. Now he has lost his wife and both of his children," said Tamsen sadly.

"The man said he would kill me," sobbed Eliza.

"He didn't mean it. Eliza was making noises. He said it just to scare her," said Frances.

"Simon says the man is crazy," said Georgia.

For Tamsen conscience and duty were often hard taskmasters, but now that duty called her, she was no longer plagued by those inner feelings of the last few days. Her duty as a neighbor and as a mother lay before her. Things had to be done now.

First she tried to air out the cabin a bit in spite of Keseberg's grumbles. She made Mrs. Murphy more comfortable. She put out bedding for airing, and searched for anything edible. The cabin seemed to have nothing. She scouted the nearest cabin, which had been the Breen's who had gone with Reed. She found one hide, a cup of beans, and an empty flour sack that yielded a little flour when she turned it inside out and thoroughly scraped it. She aired out the cabin. She decided that if she must stay the night it would be better for her and the girls to sleep in this cabin. In the morning the roads would be frozen over and easier to travel.

She found a bottle of a smelly mixture. She returned to the Murphy cabin and began the battle with the vermin.

For the girls' heads only a patient brushing and combing would be effective. Lovingly, she cleaned the girls and restored their clothes the best she could.

The next morning Tamsen was anxious to get back to George, and she got the girls ready for the trek back to the Alder Creek shelters.

She heard the shouts of men coming down from the pass. Was it Woodworth at last?

No. It was William Eddy and William Foster. They were hurrying on the trail with backpacks. There would be food in those packs for all of them. Thoughts of food come first when one was hungry. Then Tamsen was ashamed, for she realized that those eager young fathers, smiling at their final success, were coming to the tragedy of the deaths of their sons.

Eddy looked at Tamsen. Her eyes told him what she could not say in words when he asked for Jimmie.

Foster asked for Georgie. His brother-in-law Simon looked stricken as though he were somehow responsible. Mrs. Murphy sat up, and pointing to the man on the bed, screamed, "He killed Georgie. He cut up little Jimmie."

The bereaved fathers were stunned. Then Foster cursed Keseberg. Eddy leapt at the man. For a moment it seemed that he might strangle him. Tamsen cried out an unintelligible protest. Eddy pushed Keseberg back on the bed. She quieted them by repeating what the girls had said, and turned to the distribution of the food from the sacks.

She asked, "Is Woodworth coming?"

Eddy let out a string of oaths against Woodworth. Foster explained how Woodworth had journeyed with a load of supplies as far as the first camp.

"He stayed there. He was too lily-livered to get his precious feet cold or muddy," said Eddy.

Soon two more men came with packs. To Tamsen's surprise one was Hiram Miller who had driven oxen for them as far as Fort Laramie, and then had gone on to California on horseback. Tamsen felt that these men were friends.

Eddy said, "We must start back immediately. Another storm might come and catch us. Foster, you and the fellows look around and find anything we should take. Fix things to make your mother-in-law comfortable. We can't take her, but get Simon ready to go. Keseberg will have to look after himself. Mrs. Donner, I see you and your girls are all ready to go."

"Oh, Mr. Eddy, I can't go. You see, I can't leave George. Can you wait for me to go to my camp? I'll give you gold to take my girls. Clark and Jean Baptiste are staying with my husband while I'm here, but they could go with you and carry little Sammy, Aunt Betsy's little boy."

"I wouldn't take one penny of your money, even if you tried to give me thousands. Jean and Clark can take care of George. Reed told me that George was not long for this world and he had hired the men to take care of him. Anyway we are glad to take the girls. Look there. Miller is using a blanket to make a cradle so he can carry the littlest one on his back."

Just then, Thompson came from the other cabin with some oxen harnesses he had found. He took out his knife, cut strips of leather, took a sewing kit from his pack, and proceeded to make some moccasins to fit over Frances's fragile shoes.

His acts gave Tamsen a feeling of assurance.

Tamsen said, "I sent a bag of valuables--silver and silks--with the men when they took the girls. Did the men leave the bag here?"

"No, Mamma, the men took them. They even took

our food," said Frances.

"The thieving rascals!" exploded Eddy.

Tamsen asked, "Did you hear anything about Mr. Reed's party? Did they get to their first cache of food before the blizzard on March sixth?"

"Not quite. They had to make camp on the snow and wait out the blizzard. A couple of days later we met them."

"They didn't have enough food to last long. Are Elizabeth's children all right?" asked Tamsen in a rising panic as she reached for her girls and brought them under the protection of her arms.

Eddy said evasively, "Well, I talked to your niece Mary. She will be all right."

Will be. That meant that things had been bad for her. Tamsen knew that the young men were trying to withhold some information. Was it the death of Mary's little brother? Hunger and death had been with them so long, Tamsen did not ask more.

Foster said lamely, "Everything will be all right. They have plenty of supplies now."

Eddy said, "It is God's mercy that saved your little girls from taking that trip. Even this hole," indicating the cabin, "was better than being out in that storm."

God's mercy. Eddy was not particularly a religious man, but the expression seemed to resolve for Tamsen all the inner turmoil of the last eleven days.

Eddy said, "I'm glad we found you folks here. It saves us enough time to get ahead of the rising streams." Then he issued his last invitation to her personally.

Tamsen shook her head. She knew she must return to George. She must release her girls to the pattern of their lives. The strands were not in her hands to weave, and she might never know that pattern.

Eddy said regretfully, "I'll have to leave you until the next party gets here. I'm afraid Mrs. Murphy won't last that long. Keseberg's foot is too bad for him to walk on now, so he will have to wait. We'll take Simon and your three."

Tamsen kissed the girls for the last time. The four men and the four children started up the trail toward the pass. She watched them to the first bend.

She was left with her sense of rightness. She was a whole person, ready to face whatever fate lay before her.

Chapter 29

Tamsen Donner went down the trail to Alder Creek with her back to that land of glorious dreams and to the bedside of her dying husband. Her sense of rightness and wholeness was still with her. It was the rod given her when she did her duty.

The road was very slushy now and hard to travel. It was almost dark when she reached her shelter.

Jean Baptiste and Clark were nowhere to be seen. Apparently yesterday as soon as she had left the two men had gone through the chests and had taken all the silverware and coins they could find. Also they had taken two of George's guns.

Tamsen hurried to George. Beside him lay the dead body of little Sammy. He must have died during the night. She laid him in the snow beside his mother.

George greeted Tamsen with a smile, and reached out his hand for hers. She told him that his girls were safe. Then she told him that one of the rescuers was Hiram Miller who had left them at Fort Laramie to go by horseback. George nodded. He was too weak to talk.

Tamsen seldom left George's side, only occasionally taking time to fix a little food for herself. George would not eat.

For a few days George was in a coma. Tamsen sat by him or lay at his side, his hand in hers. Then one morning she woke to find he had died with his hand still in hers.

Tamsen took her best quilts, wrapped him in them, dug in the snow, and laid him away.

For days Tamsen seemed to move around automatically, pecking at little jobs. Then finally grief and tears came. The sunshine, the sparkling snow, the quiet calmness of the trees brought their healing.

At first she wanted to be alone in her grief. Then after a while she knew what she must do. There were two more people at the lake. She should be there if Woodworth should happen to come, though she no longer trusted in him. Anyway they could go on the trail.

Making a flat bundle of the bank notes that had been hidden in the quilt and taking the last scraps of food, on March 26 she started out for the lake.

She found that Mrs. Murphy had been dead a week.

Keseberg was sulky and unfriendly. Tamsen tried to persuade him to walk. She pointed out that even if rescuers came after them they would have to walk. She was sure there were now plenty of signs so they would not lose the trail. She could not persuade him.

"You'd die in the snow," he said.

Tamsen thought, *I'd rather die in the snow than in this vermin infested place.*

On Friday she started up the trail. She knew from the stories others had told it was a day's journey to the foot of the pass. They had always made camp before crossing the next morning. Tamsen found the site for the campfire and some wood left by the last party.

In the morning she faced the steep exhausting climb over the pass.

On that Saturday, March 28, the ninth and last storm began and lasted for two days.

It was not a raging snowstorm. The snow fell softly and steadily. It piled deep, obscuring the trail. It wrapped Tamsen like a shawl of eiderdown. She pressed on. Then she rested. Becoming more and more relaxed, she drifted into a phase of contentment, and then into sleep.

The End